P/99

Charteris' The ...
Hapsburg N...
M.

MYS

The Saint
and the Hapsburg Necklace

By Leslie Charteris

DAREDEVIL   THE WHITE RIDER
THE BANDIT   X ESQUIRE

The Saint Series in order of Sequence

MEET THE TIGER!

ENTER THE SAINT

THE SAINT CLOSES THE CASE

THE AVENGING SAINT

FEATURING THE SAINT

ALIAS THE SAINT

THE SAINT MEETS HIS MATCH

THE SAINT V. SCOTLAND YARD

THE SAINT'S GETAWAY

THE SAINT AND MR. TEAL

THE BRIGHTER BUCCANEER

THE SAINT IN LONDON

THE SAINT INTERVENES

THE SAINT GOES ON

THE SAINT IN NEW YORK

THE SAINT OVERBOARD

ACE OF KNAVES

THE SAINT PLAYS WITH FIRE

FOLLOW THE SAINT

THE HAPPY HIGHWAYMAN

THE SAINT IN MIAMI

THE SAINT GOES WEST

THE SAINT STEPS IN

THE SAINT ON GUARD

THE SAINT SEES IT THROUGH

CALL FOR THE SAINT

SAINT ERRANT

THE SAINT IN EUROPE

THE SAINT ON THE SPANISH MAIN

THANKS TO THE SAINT

THE SAINT AROUND THE WORLD

SEÑOR SAINT

THE SAINT TO THE RESCUE

TRUST THE SAINT

THE SAINT IN THE SUN

VENDETTA FOR THE SAINT

THE SAINT ON T.V.

THE SAINT RETURNS

THE SAINT AND THE FICTION MAKERS

THE SAINT ABROAD

THE SAINT'S CHOICE

THE SAINT IN PURSUIT

THE SAINT AND THE PEOPLE IMPORTERS

CATCH THE SAINT

THE SAINT AND THE HAPSBURG NECKLACE

Leslie Charteris'

The Saint and
the Hapsburg Necklace

written by

CHRISTOPHER SHORT

PUBLISHED FOR THE CRIME CLUB BY

DOUBLEDAY & COMPANY, INC.

GARDEN CITY, NEW YORK

1976

All of the characters in this book
are fictitious, and any resemblance
to actual persons, living or dead,
is purely coincidental.

First Edition in the United States of America

ISBN 0-385-11226-2
Library of Congress Catalog Card Number 75-14811

Contents

Contents

How Simon Templar dined alone, and was introduced to a cat

1

The restaurant of the Hotel Hofer in Vienna was called the Hofburg, presumably after the Imperial Palace of that name not very far from it. It enjoyed a certain autonomy of its own, for it was in a separate building from the hotel, although it could be reached from the latter without going out of doors. It was used as much by the general public as by the guests of the hotel. It was perhaps remarkable that anyone used it at all, for the food was poor and the service matched it. It was, however, conveniently situated in the central portion of the town, not far from the Mariahilferstrasse.

That mild rainy evening in October 1938, Simon Templar regarded it with a jaundiced eye. It struck him that although the Hofburg went in strongly for atmosphere, the management did not seem at all clear what sort of ambiance they were trying to attain. The décor was a mixture of traditional and modern. The walls were panelled with huge paintings of Austrian scenes, done in crude bright colours. They looked as if they had been executed by an enthusiastic amateur, perhaps the proprietor's wife. On the other hand, the furniture was of that varnished Swedish type which some regarded as the height of *chic* even when it also provided the height of discomfort.

Simon wondered vaguely what he was doing in the Hofburg restaurant. His thoughts expressed a mood rather than a conscious question. Factually, he knew very well why he was there. He was staying at the Hotel Hofer because that day he had had an appointment there with Van Roeper, an internationally known jewel merchant of highly elastic ethics, an appointment which at that time and in that place was curious because Van Roeper was a Jew, and the Nazis had earlier in the year taken over Austria as being rightfully a part of the primordial German State. The Saint considered this a somewhat arbitrary concept in view of the fact that the German State had only been invented by Bismarck a little over half a century before.

Even more curious was the fact that the Saint, as Simon Templar was known in many cosmopolitan circles, including both criminal and police spheres, had been the entrepreneur in a deal between the German Government and Van Roeper, which piece of pragmatism showed that Nazi racial intolerance was nothing more than totally unscrupulous opportunism. What the German Government did not know, however, was that both the Saint and Van Roeper would prosper from the transaction, whereas the Third Reich would be the loser —but that, as the saying goes, is another story.

No, the Saint was merely wondering why he was eating a bad meal in the unfashionable surroundings of the Hofburg restaurant when he could have been dining with Patricia Holm at the Savoy in London, Maxim's in Paris, or the 21 Club in New York. The simple answer was, of course, that the drizzle outside, and plans for an early departure in the morning, had made him just apathetic enough about sallying forth in search of something more epicurean or exciting. The thought of Patricia sent him into a reverie which included many pleasant and very private memories; but his preoccupation with these did not prevent him from taking note of what went on around him, particularly when this was female and unusually pretty to boot.

She came in with a certain regal swing to her carriage and sat down at the table next to Simon. She was dark with the olive skin usually associated with the Mediterranean, but her eyes were a wonderfully brilliant blue, a combination one rarely sees outside of Ireland. She looked nervous and unhappy and she appeared to be waiting for someone, for when the Herr Ober approached with the menu she shook her head, somewhat arrogantly, Simon thought.

The Saint had finished his dinner. He called for his bill and signed it, adding his room number. But he lingered on for he had nothing particular to do, and the young woman intrigued him. He wondered about her. Something was wrong, of that he felt sure. She did not fit into the Hofburg at all. She was quite a different class of person from the rest of its clientele. Of course, she might be one of the ubiquitous Nazi agents who held the Third Reich together and kept a special eye on foreigners such as himself. He would not have minded this, for so far as he knew the Nazis still had nothing on their books against him. If the girl was a Nazi agent her surveillance would be purely routine, and a report of his movements would be given to the Gestapo where it would end up in some huge and dusty filing system.

On the other hand, Austria had been a police state from way back, and if this girl was an agent of the Austrian police, the situation could be awkward. The Saint was very much wanted by the Austrian police for certain incidents in Innsbruck and the Inn valley a few years previously in which some of their stalwarts had suffered considerable violence and loss of face.* He himself had no guilty conscience about the affair, since in the beginning he had with the most laudable intentions taken them for villains just because they looked and acted like it. He had forgotten that appearances can be very deceptive and that a lot of policemen look like villains even though beneath their unrighteous exteriors may beat hearts of

* See *Saint's Getaway*.

gold; but he was bound to doubt that the Law would take such a tolerant view of his slight mistake.

It was typical of the Saint's insouciant recklessness that he hadn't even bothered to disguise himself on his return to Austria, although he had acquired, from a certain shady character in a flat above a grocery in Soho, a new character and a passport to go with it which stated that he was one Stephen Taylor, profession "gentleman" (which in those balmy days was still an officially recognised "occupation"), for whom His Britannic Majesty's Principal Secretary of State for Foreign Affairs requested and required in the Name of His Majesty all those whom it might concern "to allow him to pass freely without let or hindrance, and to afford him such assistance and protection" as might be necessary. The fine ring of this resounding injunction in its present context made Simon smile.

In taking this gamble, Simon was acting less foolishly than perhaps it seemed. False moustaches, beards, and other disguises often look unreal and are a nuisance to wear. Police photographs of wanted criminals, moreover, are not generally displayed where many people see them, and rare indeed is the individual in or out of uniform capable of recognising the original of such a portrait. Simon therefore felt fairly safe in his assumption that he was not likely to meet anyone, bureaucrat or otherwise, who would recognise him or even suspect that Stephen Taylor was not the man his passport claimed he was. In any case, he had not intended to spend much time in Austria. He had other pressing business back in London, to say nothing of dining with Patricia at the Savoy. Perhaps this time he would take her to the Ritz. He loved its *fin de siècle* French baroque restrained ostentation. Or better still, perhaps the Blue Train around the corner from it. The atmosphere there was intimate and at the same time impersonal, just the right mixture for an evening with a special person . . .

Meanwhile, however, he felt no monastic obligation to ignore anyone else of that gender who pleased the eye and the imagination.

The girl had not been sitting at her table for long before a man joined her. He was not at all the sort of person one would have expected her to be waiting for. His slight frame was encased in a raincoat, the belt of which was drawn so tightly that the coat ballooned out below it almost like a skirt. His face was narrow, and the felt hat which he did not take off when he sat down was pulled over his forehead, giving him a somewhat sinister air. His appearance reminded Simon of nothing so much as a large rat, for his skin was grey, his eyes narrow and shifty, and his mouth thinly compressed. It showed petulance rather than strength, however. When he finally did take his hat off his sinister quality largely disappeared, for he was completely bald save for some wisps of hair which stuck out clownlike from the sides of his head.

The Saint watched the couple with idle interest. The man was talking to the girl in a low voice with great urgency. At intervals she shook her head violently and even angrily. Suddenly the man stopped talking, and fixing her with an almost hypnotic look he put on his hat and stood up, becoming once more the evil-looking rat.

She sat for a moment staring at him, an expression of astonishment on her face. Then she too rose—somewhat reluctantly, the Saint thought. Pulling her coat about her she started for the door.

For a moment her eyes met the Saint's. To his surprise, they seemed to wish to say something, but he decided that that was just wishful thinking on his part. Then she was gone, probably leaving his life for ever.

The thought gave him a twinge of regret. Hotels are lonely places for men who do not have their wives or girlfriends along. Also, Simon was very choosey. A girl had to have that special quality, something exciting and unknown yet almost tangible, which made her different. This girl had it.

Simon wondered whether she and her companion were

lovers. In Vienna this would be quite possible, even though he was obviously much older than she, and a distinctly unattractive type at that. In Vienna relationships between men and women, although tinged with the romance of a Strauss waltz, were usually totally down-to-earth as well. The man could have been rich and the girl poor. Simon decided against this little fantasy, principally because he did not like the idea himself. In any case, if the Rat was rich, he was too mean to buy himself a new raincoat.

He was idly speculating about other possible reasons that might have brought this unlikely pair together when he suddenly noticed that the girl had left her handbag behind. There might still be time to catch her. He sprang to his feet, grabbed up the bag, and hurried after her.

It was blowing and raining outside. In the gloom Simon could see the figures of the man and the girl hurrying up the street towards a parked car. Huge jagged shadows chased after them, created by the swaying sign of the Hofburg restaurant. Heedless of the rain, the Saint ran after them, moving silently like a great cat. He quickly caught up with the pair.

Simon spoke fluent German, as he did a number of languages. He held out the bag towards the girl and explained how he had come by it. Her face was pale and ghostly in the half light, and her blue eyes looked almost black and seemed very large. It suddenly struck Simon that she was frightened.

"*Danke, danke vielmals,*" she said huskily.

The man grabbed her by the arm.

"*Komm!*" he commanded her roughly.

Simon noticed that he stood very close to her, pressing his body to hers in a protective fashion. Perhaps they were married after all. If that was the case he did not think much of her lot—or rather her "little." The man looked a bit of a brute, but a mean rather than a strong one.

Simon never minded out-and-out badness. In fact, it rather appealed to him as long as it was openhearted and large-minded. But petty viciousness was anathema to him. It reminded him of tax collectors, customs officials, and all the other people who wanted to spoil a free and lusty enjoyment of life.

The girl stood firm.

"*Nein. Ich muss diesem Herren danken.*"

"*Komm!*" snarled the man again, tugging at her arm. "*Wir haben uns verspätet.*"

The girl shook him off. She opened her bag and fumbled in it.

"*Hier ist etwas für Sie.*"

She handed Simon a banknote.

The Saint was irritated, understandably so. No man who has done what he considers to be a gallant act likes to be tipped for it, unless he belongs to those vocations in which tipping is a part of income. He thrust the money curtly back at her.

"I am not a porter," he told her in German.

She was finished with him however. Brushing the money aside, she turned and got into the parked car while the man held the rear door open for her. Simon saw there was another man in the driver's seat. He was bulky and had a simian appearance. The rat-faced man joined the girl and slammed the door in Simon's face. The car shot off, spattering him with rainwater from the gutter.

Cramming the banknote into his pocket, Simon walked back to the Hofburg restaurant fuming. When he got there he thought it might be soothing to have a drink and he ordered a glass of the apricot brandy which he considered to be Austria's finest beverage. When the *Barack* came, he reached into his side pocket and pulled out the banknote the girl had just given him, thinking wryly that he might as well use it to solace the pride that it had wounded.

To his surprise he noticed that it was covered with writing.

He paid the waitress with another banknote from his wallet and spread the note with writing on it out on the table. The script was in German:

*Emergency, help! Please ring U-58-331 and say that
Frankie has been kidnapped. Keep this for your trouble.*

The Saint felt an old familiar tingle of anticipation spreading through his ganglions. It was the physical confirmation of a psychic certainty. Something in his subconscious clicked and switched on that delicious anticipatory glow which assured that Adventure was rearing its lovely head. It was rather like water divining, or dowsing as the practitioners preferred to call it. One either had the extra sense or one didn't. The Saint did.

He sat thoughtfully looking at the note. How did the message come to be on it? The girl had certainly written nothing in the restaurant. Therefore it must have been prepared beforehand, as a precaution against the need for it. But why should anyone go to the extravagance of writing out a message of this kind on a banknote?

Of course, it could be that the writing was a childish prank and the girl hadn't even known it was there. But the Saint's joyous glow told him that this was not the explanation.

Well, there was one way of finding out the truth. He went through to the front lobby of the hotel where there was a public telephone, an unusual amenity in Viennese hotels. He gave the operator the number. There was a short interval and mysterious clickings, and Simon had the sensation he frequently experienced while using foreign telephones that he was quite likely to end up talking to himself. The thought occurred to him that in the new Nazi Vienna a Gestapo agent might be monitoring all telephone calls. The idea of such an invasion of his privacy irritated him, but then making telephone calls through sluggish operators back home in Britain, where there was no such supervision, irritated him too.

Then a man's voice said: "*Allo, allo, ici Radio Paris.*"

The Saint never allowed anything to take him aback. He might be surprised but he was never dumbfounded.

"*Ici Radio Luxembourg,*" he retorted. "*Prenez Bovril pour combattre le sens coulant!*"

There was a moment of silence. Then the other laughed.

"*Très comique,* but Radio Luxembourg advertises in English. You are English, no?"

"Well, actually I'm a Nigerian Eskimo," Simon replied. "I learnt my English at Eton, Borstal, and Quaglino's. But my education doesn't come into it. I have a message for you. It's from someone called Frankie."

"So?" The voice had lost its booming affability and was suddenly coldly guarded. "What is this message, then?"

"She says she has been kidnapped."

There was such a long silence Simon thought he had been disconnected. Finally the man spoke. His English, though fluent, had an unmistakable Austrian lilt.

"If you would tell me your name . . . ?"

"It is unimportant. Anonymous Bosch Unimportant, Esquire. Who are you?"

"See here, my friend!" the other snapped back. "This is serious. Her life may be in danger."

The Saint was as bland as a poker player bluffing a weak hand into a good one.

"Suppose we meet somewhere? We must have a long talk. I'm dying to catch up on all your news."

There was another pause. Then the man chuckled.

"And I should like to meet you, Mr . . . er . . . Unimportant. I admire your sense of humour. Let us arrange a rendezvous at the Edelweiss in half an hour, if you are near enough to make it. Do you know the place?"

"No, I don't, but I daresay a taxi driver will."

"They all do. And stick a piece of white paper in your lapel so I will recognise you."

"And how shall I recognise you?"

"I shall be wearing a Siamese cat," the man replied, and hung up.

2

Vienna is really two cities, the Alte Stadt, dating from the Middle Ages, and the baroque city of Maria Theresa with later additions under the Emperor Franz Joseph. To some extent the two parts mingle. The Alte Stadt is bounded by The Ring, Vienna's main thoroughfare, built in the nineteenth century on the site of the old city wall. But the baroque style of the outer city has breached this boundary in many places, and nowadays most of the medieval buildings of the Alte Stadt are to be found in the region around its shopping street, the Graben.

The Edelweiss was a small cosy restaurant in this old part of the town. It was furnished in the Tyrolean manner with plain wooden chairs and tables, and its walls were covered with unvarnished panelling.

At close on ten o'clock that night it was fairly empty. The Saint chose a central table where he could see anyone who came in yet which was in a comparatively isolated position. He tore off a corner of a newspaper he was carrying and rolled it up and stuffed it in his lapel.

He ordered an apricot brandy and sipped it while he watched the door. He wondered vaguely if he might have misunderstood the man on the telephone. Perhaps he had really said Siamese "cap" with a "p," instead of "cat," and would turn out to be an oriental gentleman wearing his national headdress.

He need not have worried. The cat lay on its owner's shoulders like a fur collar. It looked like a particularly valuable specimen of its kind.

The man saw Simon at once and made for his table. He was short, stocky and balding, with somewhat flabby features, a flat nose, and merry brown eyes. His age could have been anywhere between forty-five and sixty. He wore a green loden coat and a black Tyrolean hat, which he removed as he came through the door.

"Ach," he called out to Simon, coming over and holding out his hand. "It is good to see you, my friend Anonymous."

Simon got up and shook the extended hand.

"Is this table all right for you?" he asked.

"Excellent. There is no one within earshot."

"That's why I chose it," said Simon as they seated themselves. "What will you have to drink?"

"Six brandies. But this is my party. What are you drinking?"

"I'll stick to *Barack*, thank you—just one!" Simon said.

The waiter evidently knew the Saint's companion, for without question or comment he brought along a tray on which were six brandy glasses, each with a double measure of golden liquid in it, and a liqueur glass containing Simon's drink. He bowed and departed, a handsome tip clutched in his hand.

"Here's to you, Simon said, raising his glass.

"*Prost!*" said the other, draining the first of his brandies at a gulp. "By the way, please excuse that Radio Paris business. It is a means of letting me know who is calling."

"I don't quite see how."

"My friends who know my methods simply go right ahead and talk. Strangers apologise and hang up."

"And you never take calls from strangers?"

"Not late at night. That's when I do most of my business. I only use this trick in the evening. It didn't work with you because you are a witty man, and I like to be amused."

His cat slipped down off his shoulders and licked the inside of his empty glass. Its owner stroked its ears affectionately. "You had better look out, Thai, or you'll become a drunkard like your papa."

"If you don't mind my asking, do you always have six brandies at the same time?"

"Usually."

"Wouldn't it be more convenient just to order a bottle and pour your own?"

The other laughed. "Ah, but that would be the sign of the confirmed alcoholic. This way I know exactly how much I have had to drink." He tossed off another brandy.

Simon warmed to the man. He had a certain infectious gaiety which was cheering, especially in a Vienna which was stark with the tensions and gloomy forebodings of the time. "I take it you're not married," he said.

"No, I'm not, but why do you say so?"

"Married men don't wear cats," said the Saint. "Their wives won't let them."

His vis-à-vis tossed down his third brandy. "My name is Max Annellatt—with two 'n's, two 'l's and two 't's. Are you still shy about telling me yours?"

"Not at all, now that I've met you. It's Taylor, Stephen Taylor. I'm in the oil business."

Herr Annellatt nodded.

"A very good business too in these times. You can't fight a war without oil." He gave Simon a shrewd look. "If you are smart both sides will end up buying it from you."

"You think it will come to war, then?"

The other shrugged.

"Eventually it always comes to war, and we lose everything we have gained by making the machines to wage it. Then we have to start getting rich all over again. It is unfortunate, but it is also a fact of life. In 1922 I was broke. I literally did not have enough to buy food. Now I am a millionaire—in your currency!" He suddenly turned serious. "Now tell me, what do you know about Frankie?"

"I was beginning to wonder if we'd ever get around to that."

Annellatt laughed.

"Everything in Austria takes a long time, including living—and therefore dying!"

When Simon had finished his tale, Annellatt whistled.

"It looks bad but we will cope with it." He stubbed out his cigar. "Anyway, thank you very much, Mr . . . er . . . Taylor. You can forget about the whole thing now."

Simon was piqued by this bland dismissal, but he only smiled lazily.

"Perhaps I ought to go to the police."

The other gave him a sharp look.

"Where would that get you? If they thought there was any-thing in your story, all they could do would be to get in touch with me, and I would say I had never heard of Frankie." He caressed Thai's attenuated ears. Animal and master both wore the same expression of calm self-assurance. "Believe me, Mr Taylor, it is better for Frankie if I keep both the police and you out of this business."

The Saint did not see why this cool customer should have everything his own way. He could be pretty cool, even arc-tic, himself. Besides, he was curious to learn more about Max Annellatt and the situation in which he himself had become involved.

"As a matter of fact, I imagine you probably wouldn't be too keen yourself on the police nosing into your affairs," he remarked pleasantly.

There was a long pause. Max's eyes reminded Simon of the glacial snows on the mountains above Innsbruck. They had that same quality of cold blue timeless menace, as if their owner had existed since the dawn of history. Well, in a sense he had. Every generation has its quota of Max Annellatts. In his own way, the Saint was one of them. The thought amused him. It also pleased him. He liked dealing with peo-ple of his own calibre, and Max looked like measuring up to this.

Annellatt suddenly gave Simon a brilliant and charming smile.

"All right, what do you want to know? I should have thought you would have realised by now that the less you do know the better it will be for you."

"Well, for a start you can tell me if I'm breaking the law by not going to the police. I don't really care, but I am interested."

The other shook his head.

"No, because the police would never be able to prove that a crime has been committed." He shot Simon a knowing look. "I also am a good judge of men. I have to be in my business— in fact in order to stay alive. My intuition tells me that perhaps you too would not want the police making enquiries about you, Mr er . . . Taylor?"

Simon erupted into laughter. He was genuinely delighted. In his lonely and dangerous life he was seldom able to find such instant rapport as he had achieved with Max Annellatt. They were two of a kind.

It remained to be seen whether they were equal in quality. Simon felt sure he knew the answer to that one. But he was always pleased to meet a really formidable opponent, especially a likeable one. He rarely got a chance to stretch his own powers to the full, and even less frequently against someone he admired. Perhaps one day he would lose to someone like Max Annellatt and like it, just as he had almost lost to Crown Prince Rudolf in the same country some years before. It had been a near thing, and the Saint had liked Rudolf even when they were doing their best to kill each other. He felt the stirrings of the same sort of appreciation for Max.

"Anyway," Max continued, "you will have the comfort of knowing that you have helped a young woman in difficulties and perhaps even saved her life. Believe me, matters can be left safely in my hands."

"What sort of difficulties?" inquired the Saint. "They must be pretty big to involve kidnapping."

"I cannot tell you that without your getting involved. And for your sake, to say nothing of Frankie's, I cannot allow that."

The Saint shrugged. There was obviously no point in arguing or probing further. But what Herr Annellatt did not know was that the Saint was going to get involved anyway. His dander was up and he was not going to be fobbed off. The Saint had never in his life settled for the role of pawn. A knight, or a rook (spelt with a silent "c"?) perhaps, but never a pawn.

But he would get involved in his own way and in his own time. He got up to go.

"Well, thanks for nothing, but I've enjoyed it."

Herr Annellatt clasped Simon's hand warmly.

"Goodbye, my friend. I am so sorry you had all this bother. But do not worry, the girl will be all right."

Simon looked back over his shoulder as he went through the door. Max was finishing his last brandy. The cat was back on his shoulders. Its eyes momentarily caught Simon's.

The Saint could have sworn that Thai winked at him.

3

The Hotel Hofer was one of the new commercial hotels, still blessedly rare, which the burghers of Vienna considered to be in tune with the times.

Hotels in Vienna, for the most part, have always been noted for their old-world charm. Guests in them were treated as if they were Hapsburgian nobility, which made the Austrian aristocrats feel at home and foreigners that they were experiencing something of a culture other, and possibly higher, than their own.

In the new commercial hotels, however, guests were treated like the travelling salesmen most of them were. The emphasis was less on politeness than on efficiency. Viennese efficiency being what it has always been, the guests were the losers all round and were neither made to feel at home nor welcomed with the deference due to honoured clients. They were, in fact, as far as possible ignored by management and staff, who were in the grip of that most pathetic fallacy of the twentieth century, namely that efficiency means less work and less courtesy.

The night clerk at the Hotel Hofer appeared to be completely disinterested in his job and indeed in life itself. But then, Simon decided, being a night clerk must be rather like being in limbo and living in a half-world of demi-reality and semi-emotions.

The clerk just managed to summon up enough energy to fumble in the pigeonhole for the key to Simon's room. It was not there, and the clerk suggested bitterly, as if this was the last straw in a stack of irritations, that it must have been left in the door. Simon abandoned him to his subtle reproaches and went up in the lift, which was one of that strange Continental variety that can be said only to go upwards, since they return immediately to the ground floor without being able to stop at any stations en route. Simon could never understand why. Perhaps the theory behind them was that even someone with a weak heart or a gamey leg should, with typical Austrian reasoning, walk downstairs for the exercise.

His key was in his door. He turned it cautiously, for of one thing he was certain: he had not left it there. Some chambermaid or other hotel employee might have done so, although this was unlikely since chambermaids had master keys, and there would be no legitimate reason for anyone else to enter his room, using Simon's key to do so.

He opened the door inch by inch. The bedside light was on. From where he stood in the passage he could see the body on his bed.

It was a girl. Simon recognised her immediately. Her name was "Frankie." Or perhaps it had been up to now. Her arm hung limply down the side of the bed—and lifelessly.

But Frankie wasn't dead—just dead to the world. As the Saint closed the door behind him and approached the bed her eyes flew open, and she sat up with a gasp.

"The face is familiar," Simon said with a smile. "And I

can even put a name to it. How did you get un-kidnapped, Frankie?"

He spoke in German, but she replied in English.

"I am sorry," she said, and her voice shook slightly. "I had to come here. There was nowhere else to go."

The Saint walked over to his suitcase, unlocked it, and took out a hip flask.

"How about a little medicine? Cognac. Very special 1924 Delamain. Nice and dry." He poured the pale amber liquid into the silver top of the flasp and sniffed the aroma appreciatively. "The best way to drink it is to gargle it first and then swallow. Of course, a purist would just taste it and spit it out on the floor." He handed the drink to the girl. "But perhaps that would be a bit unladylike. Not to say wasteful. Just try sipping it."

He sat down on the end of the bed and took a swig from the flask, rolling the brandy sensuously around his tongue and swallowing it as slowly as possible.

"I hate waste, even for the purest reasons," he said. "Now tell me all."

Frankie sipped her drink, eyeing the Saint cautiously over the top of it. He guessed that she was making up her mind just how to pitch her story.

"You say there was nowhere else to go," he offered helpfully. "Not even Uncle Max's?"

She looked startled.

"So he told you his name when you telephoned him?"

"More than that, he invited me out for a drink. When I left him about half an hour ago he and Thai were knocking back brandies by the half dozen."

She laughed.

"They both drink too much."

"You're avoiding my question," Simon insisted. "Why did you come here instead of going to Max's place?"

Still the girl hesitated.

"Come on," Simon urged her brightly. "You don't have to

tell me the truth, not in Vienna! Just make it interesting. I like bedtime stories if they keep me awake."

She looked slightly baffled. She had kicked off her shoes and now she wiggled her stockinged toes and regarded them earnestly as if the exercise had some important significance.

"Do you know anything about the Imperial Crown Jewels?" she asked finally.

"Certainly. They are in the Hofburg Palace." He raised one eyebrow a fraction. "But if they're not there now don't try to pin it on me."

She laughed and stretched herself in a more relaxed fashion. The brandy and the Saint's charm were taking effect.

"Even though you are not responsible, the most important piece is missing. It is called the Hapsburg Necklace and it was never in the Hofburg Museum at all."

"Tell me more. Are you trying to sell it to me?"

She raised her chin haughtily.

"Certainly not. It is a necklace that was given to Charles V of the Holy Roman Empire in 1530 by the ruler of the Turks, who were the hereditary enemies of the Austrians. It was a peace offering but it did not work, and the war with the Turks went on for another century until Prince Eugène of Savoy finally defeated them in 1718."

"My," said the Saint admiringly, "you've certainly got it all pat. I was never any good at dates in school, not that sort anyway."

She ignored his interruption.

"It contains some of the largest cut diamonds in the world. It was once literally a king's ransom."

The Saint grinned irreverently.

"Then you could probably flog it to some film star who's trying to look like the most expensive Christmas tree in the world. How much are these baubles worth?"

"*Aber natürlich*, it is priceless! Actually, the Necklace is insured for over three million of your pounds, but that is not anything like the real value."

"In other words, quite a tidy sum. Why isn't it with the other Crown Jewels?"

"In the days of the Emperors it was always kept separate because it was so valuable. Also it was regarded as a sort of lucky charm. It had a special military guard, and one of the Court positions was Keeper of the Hapsburg Necklace. It was an hereditary post, and my father, Count Malffy, was the last man to hold it."

The Saint shot her a quizzical look.

"When the new Republican Government took over the Crown Jewels in 1918, why did they leave out the Necklace?"

"They didn't. They kept on one or two Imperial institutions. Don't ask me why. One was the famous Spanish Riding School, where the Emperor's white Lippizaner horses still perform today."

Simon nodded.

"I know. I've seen them. I never fully understood the meaning of dressage until I saw those funny hats. But what about the Hapsburg Necklace? Is your father still its Keeper, or did they move him over to the Zoo?"

The girl frowned. She plainly disapproved of his flippancy.

"He died soon after the war. I think he partly starved to death during the dreadful inflation time. I don't really remember him at all except for a vague picture in my mind of a tall handsome man in a blue and gold uniform with white stars at the collar. But perhaps I am imagining even that."

"And he was the last Keeper of the Hapsburg Necklace?"

"No. There is still one."

"Who is it?"

She drew herself up proudly.

"I am."

The Saint chuckled.

"Good for you. I'll bet you look wizard in a blue and gold uniform with stars in your eyes. Where is the Necklace now?"

She suddenly seemed withdrawn.

"It's in our family castle in Hungary, Schloss Este."

"So it's quite safe, then."

"No, it is not. Not now, anyway. Admiral Horthy took over the castle for the Hungarian Government suddenly last year. It was supposed to be used as a secret headquarters for their Intelligence, I am told, but it is really occupied by the German army and the Gestapo. I suspect also that they thought they would find the Necklace there. That's why they seized it so quickly and without warning. The German Reich is desperately in need of money. Hitler is always screaming that Germany is being economically strangled. He really took over Austria mainly to get our gold reserves, not for any sentimental reasons as an Austrian."

"Do you think they have found the Necklace?"

She shook her head.

"I'm certain they haven't. It's in a very secret place. Anyway, if they had found it, why should they try to kidnap me?"

"You think those two men were German agents?"

"Yes, Gestapo. I am sure of it. I received an anonymous letter yesterday saying that if I would come to the Hofburg restaurant at nine o'clock in the evening I would hear something to my advantage about the Necklace. I felt sure the Necklace was safe, but I wanted to find out what was going on."

Her eyes seemed to flash blue fire, which, as any chemistry student knows, is the hottest kind.

"After all, I *am* the Keeper of the Hapsburg Necklace! That nasty little man offered me a large sum of money in cash to tell him where the Necklace was. When I told him what he could do with his dirty money and his dirty self he told me he was Gestapo and was arresting me, and he pointed out that he had a gun in his pocket."

"And what about the message written on the banknote?"

She blushed like a schoolgirl. "Oh, that was just a little idea of my own. I felt rather silly about it, but it did work, *nicht wahr*? It was a precautionary measure, especially since for some days I have thought I was being followed."

"But why write the message on money?"

"One is always reading in adventure stories how people who are prisoners write notes and drop them out of windows, which seems to me most useless, for not one person in a hundred picks up and reads pieces of paper they find lying around in the street. But they always pick up money. It was a good idea, yes?"

4

"It certainly worked," said the Saint thoughtfully. "Yes, I think it was a very clever idea."

The girl looked pleased. But her face fell at his next words.

"On the other hand, you almost didn't get away with it," he said.

"Why? How is that?"

"Because I nearly gave it back to you."

"Oh, the great English gentleman doesn't like to be thought the sort of man who might accept a tip." Her eyes were mischievous. "But you kept it."

"You were gone before I could give it back to you. But speaking of English gentlemen, why are we talking English?"

"Why not?"

"I mean, why did you think I was English? When we last met I was talking what I pride myself was fluent German."

"You were." She gave him an appraising look. "But I went back to the restaurant where I'd seen you sign your bill. I got the waitress to look up the slip and give me your name and room number. I told her I was your lover. Austrians are so romantic. She did not hesitate for a minute and told me what I wanted to know."

The Saint nodded.

"But why did you come to my room instead of going straight home?"

"Because if I had gone home I might have found the Gestapo waiting for me. I live in the Malffy Palais with my mother. Everyone knows where it is."

"And what about Uncle Max? Why didn't you go to him?"

There was a pause while she eyed him speculatively.

"Shall I tell you the real reason why I am here?"

"No, no, don't be silly. Tell me half a dozen imaginary reasons. It's so much more fun. So much more *gemütlich*. So Viennese."

She laughed.

"All right, Mr Templar, then I won't tell you."

Simon raised his eyebrows.

"So now you have told me. You know who I am."

"Yes, I recognised you immediately when you handed me my bag. I did have to find out what name you were using here and your room number from the waitress, but I knew who you really were."

"How? When have you ever seen me before?"

"I've been reading about you for years, in the English papers which my mother takes. And cutting out the photos of you when they printed one. Because they always called you a modern Robin Hood, and that fascinated me. I dreamed that I might run into you some day—call it a young girl's foolishness. But then, when I had this problem, I actually wondered if I could get you to help me, and I got out the pictures again to refresh my memory. But then Max came along, and it seemed easier to take him instead. So when I saw you in that restaurant, it was like a miracle or an omen or something. I knew you were watching me and would do something if I left my bag."

"All right," he said, "supposing I am the Saint. What can I do for you now?"

"You can help me get the Necklace back."

The Saint fixed her with a long cool stare. When he wanted to he could make his eyes quite mesmeric.

"Why should I?"

There was excitement in her voice as she sensed victory.

"For a reward, and a big one at that." She looked at him sideways. "But also the fun and adventure of an enterprise which might be just the sort of thing you like."

His admission was a little quirk of the lips.

"You seem to have spotted my weakness. Danger and beautiful women—often the same thing!"

"You will help me then?"

"Perhaps. But first, tell me how you escaped."

"I was lucky. It was a typically Viennese affair. In Vienna even the Gestapo cannot be sure of operating efficiently. We got into a traffic jam outside the Opera at the end of a performance of *Tristan* with Novotna and Mayer, so you can imagine the crowds. Those two men were really stupid to go that way at that time of night. That's another reason why I think they were Germans. A true Viennese would not have done it."

"A true Viennese might do almost anything," Simon dissented. "What happened then?"

"There was a policeman standing nearby, doing nothing to help the traffic of course, and so I merely got out. There was not a thing they could do about it. They couldn't shoot me and get away. If they had tried to stop me I would have screamed, and the policeman would have had to do something about that." She looked pleased with herself. "I never saw two more frustrated people."

"Why didn't you tell the cop anyway?"

"The who?"

"The *Schupo*."

"I just wanted to get away. Anyway, he would have detained me as a witness, and nowadays in Vienna I am afraid the police are ultimately ruled from Berlin. In the end they would have had to give me up to the Germans."

"Which really means you're still not safe anywhere."

A shadow of fear darkened the girl's eyes. "You are right.

But since the Anschluss who is safe in Austria? Gestapo agents are everywhere. One cannot even trust one's friends."

"What about Max Annellatt?"

Her expression was oddly secretive and she tossed the hair back from over her eyes in a gesture which was almost dismissive.

"Oh Max, he's all right. He's a very good sort really. Just a little eccentric."

"He seemed to me a little nuts."

"Nuts?"

"Mad. Crazy."

"No, he is not mad, he just carries being Austrian to an extreme."

The Saint got up.

"It comes to the same thing. Anyway, I think we'd better get you back either to him or your dear old white-haired mother, knitting in that rocking-chair in the Malffy Palace."

His words amused her.

"If you knew my mother! She's out every night with a different admirer. Admittedly some of them are gigolos, but she has fun."

"Good for her," smiled the Saint. "Remind me to look her up sometime. I like swinging *Erstegesellschaft* mums. Well, which is it to be, her or Uncle Max?"

She looked at him from under her lids.

"Wouldn't it be safer for me to stay here?"

"No, it wouldn't," the Saint told her with candour. "Besides, I want my beauty sleep. I need it even if you don't."

She pouted.

"You Englishmen are all the same. I don't think you really like women."

"No man in his senses does. Loving them is a different matter. But come on, make up your mind. It's after midnight. I'll run you round in my car."

She thought it over. "I think it had better be Max. As I said, they may be waiting for me outside the Palais. I don't think they know yet about my connections with Max. Besides, he'll be worrying about me."

The Saint looked sceptical.

"I don't think he'll be in a condition to be worrying about anything by this time."

"Oh, Max never gets drunk. It's only Thai that does. But anyway, I want to tell him that I have enlisted you in our cause."

He shook his head.

"Don't rush me. I haven't promised anything yet. Anyway, what's his part in all this?"

"He's one of the richest men in Austria and has connections everywhere. A very useful man, and a very charming one. Unfortunately my mother does not like him, but she is a snob, and he was born a peasant."

The Saint reached out his hand and helped her to her feet. "All right, we'll deliver you to Uncle Max and all his connections. But don't get ideas. I haven't said I would help you yet. I've got rather a lot on my platter just at the moment. And don't forget, Austria is not a very healthy place for me."

She gave him a mischievous look.

"I think we can count on you. I don't think you would want to miss an adventure like this one."

Simon eyed her with respect. She evidently had good reason for her self-assurance.

The Saint had borrowed Monty Hayward's M.G. N-type Magnette, for the trip—his own Hirondel was too well known, not necessarily to the Austrian authorities, nor even the German, but to the British. It would certainly have been noticed if he put it on the cross-Channel ferry, and its departure reported to the ever-suspicious attention of his old friend and enemy, Chief Inspector Teal of Scotland Yard, who had an irritating habit of trying to spoil the Saint's fun whenever he could.

The drive to Max's, with the girl giving him directions, was uneventful. They were apparently not followed, and the traffic at that hour was light, so their journey was quick.

Max Annellatt had a flat in a large baroque house in the aristocractic district behind the Belvedere Palace. The Saint got out and held the door open for Frankie.

"Well, *auf Wiedersehen.* I'll be seeing you around."

"No, you must come in and talk to Max now."

He shook his head firmly. "I've had enough of Max for tonight, charming though he is. Anyway, he's probably had enough brandy by now to send him to sleep."

"All right," she said. "But can I call you in the morning?"

"Certainly. But don't leave it too late, because I'd figured on being on my way out of here after breakfast, and you still haven't altogether convinced me that I ought to change my plans."

"Of course, I still must discuss with Max—"

"—before you take me into full partnership. I'd guessed that. So go into your huddle."

"My what?"

"Forget it, my love," he said. "This isn't the time and place for my lecture on the complexities of the English language since it became American. Nighty night, sleep tight, and mind the Gestapo don't bite."

She blew him a kiss and took a key out of her bag. With it she opened a small door which, in the fashion of large Viennese houses, was set in the frame of a much more imposing portal. She turned to say farewell, and suddenly her eyes widened as she looked over the Saint's shoulder.

Spinning around, he saw at once the cause of her alarm. Two men in raincoats had come out of the night and were standing just behind him.

One was small and rat-like, and the other looked like a gorilla.

The smaller man held a revolver.

II

How Frankie laid down the law, and the
Saint was driven into the country

1

The Saint's mind moved with lightning speed and the Saint's response was almost simultaneous. In another virtually continuous about-turn he flung himself at the girl, sending her flying through the door.

The impetus of his charge carried him through with her, and he slammed the door after him. The two men had been so surprised by his instantaneous reaction that they had not even moved.

The Saint helped Frankie to her feet. She smoothed her skirt and batted her eyelids up at him.

"You certainly do have the caveman approach."

"And you're like all women who want to make quite sure that they're looking nice even if they may get killed the next minute. Come on, let's get to Max's before they shoot the lock in. I don't think they'll risk the noise, but with these types you never know."

They were standing in a sort of archway leading to an inner courtyard of what had once been a large palais. Like so many big Viennese houses it was no longer tenanted by impoverished aristocratic owners and had been converted to flats. Without a word Frankie ran to a side door in the courtyard, which she opened with another key.

They passed through into a large almost pitch-dark entrance hall. A wide flight of bare stone steps led upwards, and Simon followed the girl up them. On the first landing she paused and opened a door with yet another key. The Saint stopped for a moment and listened but there were no sounds of pursuit. Their enemies had probably decided that it would not be politic to break down the outer door. After all, even Gestapo agents would have to explain their actions to aroused tenants and the police if they were called, and apparently for some reason the present exercise was one that they had been ordered to carry out with great discretion.

Simon followed Frankie through the door and closed it after him. The change from the bleak stone of the stairway and landing was dramatic. They were now in a long passage, thickly carpeted and hung with portraits lit by indirect lighting. The baroque plaster-work of the walls and ceiling was scrolled and touched with gold leaf, and the air was warm and comforting. Several doors opened off this wide hallway. They were big and stately, with ornamented panels and heavy gilded door-knobs.

Simon knew that the post-war housing laws in Vienna were very strict, and no owner, unless he could show good cause, or was very influential, was allowed to have more than a certain number of untenanted rooms in his premises. He guessed that Max was probably one of the privileged and that there were no "lodgers" in these several rooms.

At the end of the passage was a wide double door. Frankie opened it without knocking, and they passed through into a large handsomely furnished drawing-room, brilliantly lit by a chandelier and wall sconces. All the lights were on, as if to push more than just darkness from every corner. One felt that anything unpleasant or even disturbing could not breach the security of this room.

A blazing wood fire in the hearth made the room come alive with its variegated lights. Max was sitting in a chair by it, the Siamese cat on his lap.

He looked up as they entered. For a moment he appeared startled. Then he gave a cry of pleasure.

"Frankie, *Gott sei dank!*"

He leapt to his feet and Thai cascaded to the floor. The cat gave them all an affronted look and jumped up on to a sofa where he sat glaring distrustfully.

Max's eyes met those of the Saint.

"Ah, Mr er . . . er . . . Taylor. How delightful to meet you again! As a tourist, you certainly get around Vienna!"

Frankie moved quickly to the fire and held out her hands towards the comforting blaze.

"They are downstairs," she told Max in German.

"Who?"

"The men who kidnapped me. I think they are Gestapo."

Max glanced at Simon.

"I think it would be polite to our guest to speak English," he said in that tongue.

The girl followed suit.

"If you like, but he speaks fluent German. Max, may I introduce Mr Simon Templar, otherwise known as the Saint?"

For a long while Max stared at Simon. Then he gave a low whistle.

"So, we are indeed honoured!"

"The pleasure is all mine," Simon replied blandly. "I've had a very entertaining evening. And I find the Gestapo adds a new dimension to life."

Max grimaced.

"It certainly does! Unfortunately it is not such a nice one. Anyway, you will have a whisky while you are here, no?"

"Not no," said the Saint. "Yes, thank you very much."

He sat down next to Thai on the sofa and accepted the drink which Max brought him. The cat looked at the whisky with interest, his ears pricked, as if inviting the Saint to give him a sip.

There was a sudden noise as the door was flung open. A young man entered.

He was slightly built, slim, and he moved gracefully with an impression of controlled strength. His thick black hair was brushed smoothly straight back and his tanned face was aquiline and aristocratic.

"Frankie!" he cried when he saw the girl. "*Wie bist du denn entflohen? Ich habe die ganze Zeit nach dir gesucht seit wir deine Botschaft bekamen!*"

He walked swiftly over to the girl, taking both her hands in his. He kissed one of them and then her cheek. She looked into his eyes and smiled. There was obviously a close bond between them.

Turning towards Simon she spoke in English.

"I owe my life to our friend here. He just rescued me from the Gestapo. Mr Templar, may I introduce Count Leopold Denksdorff, my cousin?"

Simon's name apparently meant nothing to the young man, who bowed curtly.

"How do you do?" he said formally.

His English, like Frankie's, though heavily accented was excellent. Most Austrian aristocrats, as Simon knew, felt a close affinity to the English and, even after having been their enemies in a terrible conflict, emulated them whenever possible.

The Saint ignored young Denksdorff's brusque manner.

"I won't be sending a bill," he said pleasantly. "Frankie's thanks are more than enough."

Max intervened tactfully.

"Tell us the story of your escape, Frankie."

He and Leopold listened attentively to Frankie's vivid account of her adventures, and explaining Simon's part in them. The Saint observed the others closely, assessing them and their relationships. They seemed to be completely at home with each other in spite of their different temperaments and the fact that Max Annellatt's background was quite different from that of the two young aristocrats. This camaraderie was surprising even in the new democratic Austria. Habits of over a thousand years die hard, and the Austrian nobility were still a very cliquey lot.

When she had finished, the girl turned towards Simon.

"But all is well. Mr Templar is going to help us to get the Necklace. I have told him where it is." She gave Simon a dazzling smile. "He will give us a plan."

Flirting is an essential part of every Viennese girl's upbringing, but Max looked astonished.

"Was that wise, my dear? After all, you haven't even told us."

Frankie gave him a guilty glance. "I mean, I—"

"We can be grateful to Mr Templar for what he has done," the young Count interrupted rudely, "but he can be of no further use. He is not one of us."

There was a wealth of hauteur in his manner and the implication that unless one were born an Austrian aristocrat one was not properly born at all.

The Saint was only amused by the churlishness of an arrogant and probably jealous youth.

"You are quite right," he said benignly. "And every time I'm reminded of it I feel I should go on a Diet of Worms."

Max Annellatt held up a hand.

"Leopold, you must understand that Simon Templar is no ordinary Englishman. He is known as the Saint and is an international . . . er—"

"Crook?" suggested the Saint helpfully.

For the first time Annellatt looked slightly flustered.

"No, no! Perhaps 'operator' would be a better word."

"Makes me sound as if I manned a switchboard," Simon remarked. "What about Boy Scout?"

"I think I prefer 'gentleman adventurer,'" Frankie said.

"Anyway," Max said firmly, "I am in agreement with Leopold about one thing, Mr Templar. We cannot ask you to help us in our venture. It is too dangerous and it would not be fair to you."

"Keep it up and you'll really hook me," said the Saint.

"Tell me it's dull and entirely law-abiding and I'd be delighted to stay out. But dangerous, well, that's quite something else. My doctor told me I should have at least one adventure a day to keep him away. We've had today's, but there's always tomorrow."

Frankie moved swiftly over and kissed him lightly on the cheek.

"You are a dear!" she cried. "I knew you'd agree to join us in the end."

"No!" exclaimed Leopold, looking as if he were about to stamp his foot with rage. "I won't have it! Mr Templar is English. He knows nothing about Austria and nothing about us."

"I expect I could muddle through," Simon offered modestly. "It's a tradition in my country. We always win in the end. Admittedly we give a lot of people a few nasty turns en route. But we do win, even if it means just not losing."

Max's face was impassive.

"With all respect to you, Mr Templar, and with gratitude for the help you have already given us, I think Leopold is right. We simply must not impose on you any further. It would do neither you nor us any good."

His voice and manner were friendly but the Saint detected an odd undercurrent of nervousness.

Frankie suddenly drew herself up. Her face was pale but her carriage was regal.

"I wish Mr Templar to help us," she announced flatly. "It is *I* who am the Keeper of the Hapsburg Necklace, not you Leopold, nor you Max. This is *my* decision to make, and I have made it."

Her two countrymen looked at her in astonishment. There was nothing that they could say. Apparently her case was unanswerable, but they had obviously never before seen her assert herself so imperiously.

"All right," said the Saint cheerfully. "If Frankie's the boss, I can't turn down the job. '*Ce que femme veut, Dieu le veut'*—as my dear old grannie used to say whenever they tried to stop her having another double gin. So let's stop bickering and let me in on the rest of the plot. The readers are getting impatient."

2

"Just for a start," said the Saint, "I'd like to get straight on a point of protocol. Frankie, as we call her, has told me about her father, Count Malffy, the hereditary Keeper of the Necklace. Now, if I should have to ask for her somewhere else, or introduce her formally, what do I call her? Did she inherit the title as well as the job?"

"My cousin Francesca," Leopold said proprietorially, and with undisguised disdain for such ignorance, "is the *Gräfin*— Countess—Malffy."

"But the name has a Hungarian sound. How did Graf Malffy get so well in with the Hapsburgs?"

"Perhaps you did not learn in school that before the war of 1914 this was a country called Austria-Hungary."

"Oh yes, so it was. And now Hitler has made this part Germany-Austria. Well, that's life in the Balkans. Never mind. One day Hungary could be back under the same flag—if someone else doesn't grab it first."

The Countess Malffy was nobly trying to conceal her malicious delight in this sparring. But she was sensible enough to break it up again before it got out of hand.

"We are wasting time," she said. "And Mr Templar—"

"Since we're all friends, you can call me Simon."

"—Simon has a right to know how difficult is the project in which we are asking him to engage."

"As I understand it," said the Saint, "the Necklace has just been left somewhere in the ancestral Schloss."

Max went over to a beautifully inlaid Empire desk. From a

drawer he picked out a folded sheet of paper which he spread out on top of the desk.

"Here is a map of Schloss Este," he said, beckoning Simon.

The Saint walked over and looked at the map. Max's finger pointed out its details.

"Here you can see," he said, "the Germans have fortified the whole area around the Castle. It amounts to some two hundred hectares, or about five hundred of your acres."

"Not mine," Simon disclaimed. "I don't own a single rod, pole, or perch."

"This area included both the Castle and a small village of just a few houses and a church. They have put barbed wire fencing round the perimeter and an electrical fence as well. There are also sentry platforms at intervals and searchlights for use at night. They may even have mined certain vulnerable places—I'm afraid I haven't yet been able to find that out."

"But I take it you have made a thorough survey of the Castle and its environs—from the outside?"

Max nodded.

"*Aber natürlich,* I and my men have observed it all. In the daytime through high-powered binoculars, and at night we have even crossed the river which runs past one side of the fortifications, looking for some way through the barbed wire and electrical fences. One of my men thought he had found it but he was mistaken, unfortunately." He shrugged. "I had to give his widow a pension. She's really better off. She has a steady income and no husband. That's the best situation a woman can be in, so my married girlfriends tell me."

"I must remember to give you the names and addresses of my four wives—I should have warned you that I was a Moslem," murmured the Saint. "So it seems that all we have to do is cross the river at night, avoid the searchlights, get over electrical and barbed wire fences, and be careful not to step on any mines that may be lying around. All we need is a few crocodiles in the river to make our fun complete."

Max laughed.

"I told you I liked your sense of humour, Mr Templar. I see now that it can also be what we call the gallows kind."

"It may sound funny," Simon said, "but it strikes me quite seriously that to try to get into that fortified area would be rather like putting our heads in a noose."

Max shook his head. "It would be but for one thing. The Germans put up their fortifications in a hurry. What they have overlooked is that this whole valley"—his fingers traced the contours on the map—"between these hills is drained by a very large pipe buried deep in the earth. It is big enough for a man to crawl up and it comes out into the river. It was necessary because otherwise at certain times of the year when the heavy rains come the whole valley would be flooded because it lies between these two ridges of hills which run up to the Castle on either side. As you can see, the terrain forms a sort of funnel with the Castle at one end and the river at the other."

"You can't tell me the Germans haven't spotted that one," Simon objected.

Max maintained his opinion.

"It may seem strange, but they don't appear to have. After all, the exit on to the river is well hidden by shrubs and rocks, and anyway the Germans haven't been there very long. Given time they may find it, but they haven't yet. One of my men has been quite far into the drain. He found a manhole but did not dare go any farther. He was brave, but not brave enough, which is as bad as being a coward."

"So that leaves me to be the hero who opens up that manhole and sees what's on the other side. It could be that your man wasn't so much afraid as just being sensible. You expect me to be both brave and foolhardy. Well, I'm a gambler and I might take the risk. But I'll have to decide that myself if and when I get there."

Max nodded approvingly.

"Good! I at least assessed your own courage correctly."

He pointed again to the map.

"I have worked out where this manhole comes up. It comes out, as would be expected, in the middle of some agricultural land, which is the most important part of the valley to drain. There are a number of wooden sheds in that area where the farmers keep their tools and the like. Probably one of these sheds hides the entrance to the manhole to cover it against corrosion by the weather or being blocked and covered with earth. If it doesn't, the ground will almost certainly have been ploughed up all around it, and it will be in the middle of a wheat field or long grass."

"And you really will take care of all my widows?"

"I hope that will not be necessary. I think you will be quite safe. For one thing, I doubt very much that the Germans have even dreamed about the possibility of the drain's being where it is. After all, only country people know that agricultural fields are often drained by underground pipes. To most people a field is just a field and they never think what goes on underneath it. For another, no one would expect to have such a *large* drain in that place unless they knew about the possibility of flooding in that particular area because of the hills."

"But surely they must have seen the end which opens on to the river? One thing you must say for the Germans is that they may be a bit plodding and often thick-headed, but they're always thorough."

Max shook his head vigorously.

"No, it is highly unlikely, otherwise my man would never have got as far as he did. As I have told you, the exit is concealed by rocks and is overgrown with bushes. The farmers never had any reason to keep that end of the drain exposed. Flood waters coming down the pipe would spill out over anything or sweep it out of their way. A few bushes and rocks would make no difference once the waters had got that far, and if they did, the peasants could always clear them away."

"Do tell me some more cosy reasons why the drain is so absolutely safe for me to go into?" Simon smiled.

Max smiled back at him.

"The best reason is that it won't be you who goes through it first, it will be one of my men."

"And then *his* widow gets a pension, I suppose," said the Saint. "No, thank you. You're just trying to get out of this on the cheap—one widow to take care of instead of four. But I never employ stunt men. If anyone goes through that manhole first, it'll be little me."

Frankie and Leopold had been listening all this time in silence, Leopold with visible impatience, but leaving Annellatt to do all the exposition. But now Frankie leaned forward eagerly in the chair she had taken.

"Now you know all we can tell you, Simon, you are still with us?"

Simon had already made up his mind. He was, after all, a gambler at heart, albeit one who never took more chances than he had to. But your born gambler has to take some chances, and they are usually big ones. A toss of a coin with death was the sort of hazard that appealed most strongly to the Saint.

"I'm with you," he said calmly. "But I'd hate to break up a beautiful comradeship. If Max doesn't accept it, I'd be a bad risk."

Max Annellatt spread his hands generously.

"I have accepted," he said. "I too do not want a bad risk. Now I think we should all go to my country place. Would you go back to your hotel, please, Simon—pay your bill and collect your things and come back here?"

"Certainly," Simon replied. "But I like sleeping raw, and all I really need is a glass of salt water to bung my false teeth into."

Frankie giggled.

"I don't imagine you have any falsies," she said.

The Saint grinned at her.

"I shall have to give you some lessons in American slang," he murmured. "But the same to you, and thanks for the compliment. I wish I could say thanks for the memory. Perhaps I shall one day."

The girl looked mischievously pleased. In spite of his youth, Leopold appeared about to have a stroke.

"Why pay for a room if you're not using it?" Max argued practically. "Besides, it would be better if you seemed to make a normal departure, instead of just disappearing. Tell the hotel you are driving to Italy, which is the opposite direction from where we shall be going."

"You seem to have forgotten," Simon remarked, "about the Gestapo boyos lurking outside."

"There is another way out of this building," Max told him, "through the former stables, which are now garages, on to a different street, which the Gestapo should not have discovered yet. And I will lend you a car."

"Well, what about the car I came here in?" Simon objected. "It belongs to a friend of mine, and he's rather attached to it."

"So much the better, if the papers are not in your name. He can report it stolen, and in due course the police will return it to him."

The Saint drew a long decisive breath.

"Okay, Maximilian," he said. "Let's get the show on the road."

With a brief wave of temporary farewell to Frankie and Leopold, he followed Max out of the room.

Max led him down a different stairway, which nevertheless brought them to another angle of the central courtyard. The place was probably a warren of such private staircases, designed in a more spacious age so that guests and servants could move about without unnecessarily encountering each other. And it was only to be expected that a man like Max Annellatt would have provided himself with at least as many bolt-holes as a prudent rabbit.

After making sure that the courtyard was deserted, Annellatt beckoned the Saint out and led him across to the back, where another door admitted them to a dimly lit grey-walled passage which zigzagged past a few other unpainted doors and a couple of square black caves stacked with unidentifiable shrouded relics, to bring them into an equally dim-lit architectural cavern where the damp air still seemed to incorporate ineradicable nuances of its former equine occupants.

In one of the converted stalls, Max introduced him to a gleaming Mercedes-Benz 540 supercharged coupé and handed him a key.

"Do you know how to drive it?"

"I could hardly miss," said the Saint. "As I recall it, the gear box is synchro-mesh, and semi-automatic between third and fourth. To be very exact, the engine is actually 5401 cc—"

"Good," Annellatt said approvingly. He went over to a large sliding door across from the stall, unbolted it and hauled it aside. It opened on to a dark rain-washed alley, where he indicated a turn to the right. "That will bring you back to the street in front of the building, but if you turn left there you will not have to pass the entrance again and anyone who is watching it, and you will be going towards the Mariahilferstrasse. Will you remember the rest of the way?"

"Some of my ancestors," the Saint reassured him, "were homing pigeons."

"Then you should be back here within ninety minutes. Tap on this door and I shall be waiting for you."

Simon had only slightly exaggerated his sense of direction and his talent for noting and memorising routes. He found his way unerringly back to the Hotel Hofer, where it took him only a few minutes to pack the minimal travel bag which was all he had with him.

A bored night clerk seemed unsurprised at his checking out at such an hour, which might not have been so extraordinary for a commercial hotel, and gave him vague directions to the main roads towards Italy. It was not until much later that he noticed that "Mr Taylor" had filled in his forwarding address on the conventional form as "The Vatican, Rome."

He found his way just as efficiently back to the building which housed Annellatt's apartment, but parked the Mercedes short of the back alley and walked in to the sliding garage door. It was a few minutes less than the ninety that Max allowed him, and there was no response when he tapped on the door.

After a brief wait, he tried pulling the door aside, and it moved with no more resistance than its own ponderous suspension. But all was now darkness in the garage.

Simon stepped inside, reaching into a pocket for the pencil flashlight that he carried as automatically as a fountain pen. There had to be a light switch somewhere near by, if he could find it, to turn on the illuminations for late-homing tenants, otherwise some benighted elderly reveller returning from his favourite *Weinstube* might trip over a Volkswagen and get hurt.

Simon Templar was not exactly an elderly reveller, but he still got hurt. His whole world suddenly exploded and left him falling into blackness.

3

When he came to, he was in pitch darkness. For a few moments because of the discomforts of his accommodation he thought he was in his hotel bed until he realised that he was lying on a cold bare floor with his wrists tightly bound behind him. "No," he said to himelf, as cheerfully as he could in the circumstances, "I never tie myself up before going to bed. Someone's been a bit naughty."

He tried to loosen his bonds, but they were tied firmly enough to tell him that it would take even his escapologist's skill quite some time to get out of them.

Then that attempt had to be deferred as a key turned in a lock, a door was opened, and the room was flooded with harsh light from a naked bulb switched on overhead.

It was a small grey room about the size of a prison cell, which it depressingly resembled, and as he rolled over he saw that it was devoid of furniture.

Two men entered. Both wore raincoats and turned-down Trilby hats. The Saint recognised them at once. They were the Rat and the Gorilla. The names of convenience that he had given them could not have fitted more neatly. They were two perfect stereotypes from a C-grade film.

The Rat spoke in English. He had a heavy and rather guttural accent blended with that of the American locality where he had learned it, which sounded rather like Yonkers. And Simon had no doubt that in the same school he had acquired some of the less attractive characteristics of the American culture.

"So you are awake already?" he said.

As a remark it was superfluous, but it helpfully told the Saint that he could not have been knocked out for long.

Simon looked at him with distaste. The man had the sneering manner of a professional sadist. Such types, in the Saint's experience, were always vulnerable. Compensating for their own physical inadequacy with another man's muscle, they were always aware of their dependence and made more insecure by it.

"I'm not sure," Simon replied, his gaze meeting the other's steadily. "I could be having a particularly nasty dream."

"Perhaps you won't be quite so fresh, my friend, when we've finished with you," said the Rat.

"And what exactly is it you want to finish?"

The Rat lit a cigarette.

"We want to know what you are doing in Vienna."

"I came to see the Zoo," Simon told him. "But I didn't know the animals were wandering around loose in the streets."

The Gorilla stepped over and kicked the Saint viciously in the ribs. Simon could not quite cut off a reflex gasp of pain, but managed to turn it into a laugh.

"There's a good Nazi," he observed. "Be sure a man isn't only down but has his hands tied before you kick him."

The Gorilla's face was suffused with rage. He bent down and deliberately struck the Saint across the face. He looked as if it made him feel a little better.

"You must have practised that on your girlfriend," said the Saint. "Or is she a boy?"

The Gorilla reached in his pocket and brought out a switch knife. The blade flicked out like a silver snake's tongue. He thrust the point to within half an inch of the Saint's left eye.

"How would you like to have only one eye?" The blade twitched sideways. "Or no eyes at all?"

"Listen," said the Rat. "We know that you did not meet the Countess Malffy or Herr Annellatt before tonight. But the Saint wouldn't come to Vienna, at this time, just as a tourist. We want to know what you came to do, if you have already done it, and all about it."

"Und ve haf vays off making you talk," said the Saint, in contemptuously exaggerated burlesque.

"You will also tell us exactly where the Hapsburg Necklace is hidden."

So that was part of it. They thought that Frankie might have confided her secret to him. That could make things more difficult. Ignorance is one thing which is more easily shown up than it is proved. And this pair looked as if they would take a lot of convincing.

"I'm sorry," said the Saint, "but I keep my tiara in the bank and only wear paste. One meets so many unpleasant characters around these days. After all, a girl doesn't want to risk losing her most precious souvenirs."

The Rat sighed dramatically, but moved his head negatively in reply to the Gorilla's expectant glance.

"There are better and more painful ways to persuade him," he said in German. "But not here. And I see that it will take time. Blindfold him, while I see if the car is here."

He went out, closing the cell door after him. Simon Templar, whose faculties never stopped working when they were not concussed, automatically wondered about the *"not here."* A cell such as he was in would have seemed quite satisfactory for what is politely called "intensive interrogation." A change of venue could only suggest a lavishly equipped chamber of horrors which it was not amusing to imagine.

The Saint had no delusions about the power of painful persuasion. Eventually any human being would break: it was only a question of human willpower against scientifically applied agony. And in that unequal contest, science had always been ahead.

The Saint wondered what his own threshold of surrender would be. And what made the outlook exceptionally gloomy was that they would be seeking information which even in the most abject extreme he would be totally unable to give them.

It was the kind of situation which eliminated any rational scruples against the means to combat it.

The Gorilla hauled Simon to his feet like a rag doll, pulled out a dirty handkerchief, and twirled him around. He stood squarely behind Simon to tie the folded handkerchief over the Saint's eyes.

Simon reached back, at first cautiously and gently, with his bound hands, and located the Gorilla's crotch and testicles. He closed one hand on them, in a clamp like a fiercely activated vise.

The Gorilla shrieked aloud, and released the cloth he had been knotting and everything else.

Simon whirled around, keeping his balance as adeptly as a dancer. The Gorilla was bent double, clutching his anguished organs. This callisthenic exercise brought his head down to waist level. The Saint, poised on one foot, kicked it like a football, with compound interest for the kick which he himself had received.

The Gorilla instantly stopped screaming, and crumpled into blissful anaesthesia.

Simon Templar dropped to his knees, and somewhat laboriously, as it had to be with his hands tied behind him, located the Gorilla's switch knife. After that, it took him less than a minute to cut the cords from his wrists.

So far, so good! The Saint flexed his muscles and massaged the circulation back into his arms. All he had to do now was to get through the locked door and out of a building whose plan was unknown to him, and past any guards who might be still around. The thought of these obstacles made him feel quite pleased with his situation. He only hoped he would meet the Rat on his way out. He wanted to give him an object-lesson in the perils of arrogance that was not sustained by personal prowess in the arts of self-defence. It should be possible to get this into his head, even without surgery, perhaps by throwing him out of a convenient window or down a staircase. Viennese staircases are usually very long, winding, and particularly hard, being made of stone.

He was not daunted by the unknown quantity of other Gestapo cohorts whom he might encounter. At that hour, there were likely to be very few on duty, and a free and untrammelled Saint would certainly be able to cope with a couple of Nazi-type thugs, especially as he would have the advantage of the element of surprise. To paraphrase the poet, his strength was as the strength of ten, not for the reason that his heart was all that pure, but just because it was. Even though he was no Sir Galahad, he was never awed by being to some extent outnumbered. And now, thanks to the Gorilla's knife, he was not even unarmed.

His ears had told him that the Rat had not locked the cell door when he left, and in fact there would have been no reason to do so. Simon opened it cautiously, and stepped out into a dimly lit grey-walled corridor.

He had hardly stepped out when he recognised it.

It was the passage through which Annellatt had led him from the courtyard of the apartment building to the garage. The "cell" which he had escaped from lay behind one of the unpainted doors which he had seen in passing, and must have been some kind of former store-room.

The Rat and the Gorilla must have thrown him in there simply for temporary storage. And this explained why they could not use it for a prolonged "interrogation," and the Rat's reference to a car which had apparently been sent for.

It also disposed of Annellatt's rash statement that they would not have discovered the connection between the garage and the residential building.

Having found his bearings, the Saint was faced with an immediate decision: to continue his escape through the garage, or to return to the flat and warn the others—if it wasn't already too late for that . . .

It took him exactly two seconds to choose the latter. Whatever the risk, he couldn't make good his own getaway without knowing what had happened to Frankie.

He retraced the passage through the door to the central courtyard. Its baroque splendour was silent and deserted.

The door to Annellatt's principal stairway was locked. Before ringing the bell beside it, he tried to recall the position of the other door by which Annellatt had brought him out. This was a little more difficult, but he thought he located it correctly, and tried the handle.

Either by accident or design, it was not locked.

But he had barely moved the door the necessary minimum of millimetres to discover this when there was a creak of hinges from the building's main entrance. Turning his head, he saw the inset door starting to open. It might only be another perfectly innocent tenant coming home, but the Saint could not take a chance on it. With the silent stealth of a bashful ghost, he backed off so that one of the courtyard's massive marble columns was between him and the incomer.

Pressing himself tight against the pillar, and tracking the other's progress by the echoing sound of his footsteps, Simon kept himself completely hidden until his ears told him that the man had passed and was moving away from him. Only then did he come from behind his cover and see the back of a short figure in a raincoat and hat which he felt sure of recognising.

He stepped out of cover, caught up in three soundless strides, and collared the man around the throat in the crook of his left arm. In a simultaneous movement, he brought the Gorilla's knife, in his right hand, into full view before his captive's face.

"*Halb so wild*," he advised gently. "Didn't you just say we had something to finish?"

The man's hat, at first knocked over his eyes by the stranglehold, fell off completely, and the Saint found himself looking down at the unmistakable, even from that awkward angle, snub-nosed pudding features of Max Annellatt.

4

"Pardon me," said the Saint politely, releasing him. "But for a moment I thought you were someone else. Is Frankie upstairs?"

"No, I sent her off with Leopold soon after you left, in his car. To the Malffy Palais, to pack a bag and go straight on to my country place. I promised her we would join them there."

"Why weren't you in the garage to meet me?"

"I went with them to the Palais, to be sure it was not under surveillance. I don't think Leopold would have known what to do if it had been. Then it took me an infernal time to get a taxi to bring me back. I apologise for being late—but how did you get in?"

"Those lads from the Gestapo let me in, and coshed me before I could find out they weren't you."

Max's eyes widened.

"Then they have found out about the garage! But it must have been since we left." He glanced apprehensively across the courtyard at the door to the passageway. "But you—"

"I managed to get away, by a trick which would have horrified the Marquis of Queensbury. If not his son. But even if one of them isn't in top form at the moment, we'd better not spend any more time nattering here."

"I saw you had left my car up the street, as I came in the taxi," Annellatt said. "And now you have explained to me why no one was watching the front of the building. Let us take advantage of it before they realise that two people can be in two places at once."

"You took the words out of my mouth," said the Saint.

They crossed quickly to the front door, which Max opened and pre-empted the first step out—"As a resident here, I have every right to come and go as I please." But the street outside was deserted.

They hurried along to the next block, where Annellatt headed authoritatively for the door on the driver's side and opened it. The Saint just as naturally accepted the passenger position. He found that he still had the ignition key, and handed it over.

"She goes well, doesn't she?" Annellatt said as he started the engine. "But it was careless of you to leave the doors unlocked, especially with your luggage in the car. You should never leave things in unlocked cars in Vienna. The inhabitants of this town are strictly honest, but that doesn't stop them stealing and cheating the tax inspectors. Only the Viennese can be moral and immoral at the same time."

"That isn't just Viennese, it's an Austrian national characteristic," Simon permitted himself to generalise. "But if you take that personally, I hope it's in the nicest way."

Max seemed to take no umbrage. There was a slight smile on his lips as he kept his eyes on the road. One would not have taken him for a rally driver, but he handled the Mercedes impeccably.

"Would you like to tell me now how you escaped?"

Simon filled him in briefly on the details.

"My head still aches," he concluded, "but I think the Gorilla will be aching a bit longer."

"It will not make him more friendly if you ever meet again," Annellatt opined. "Let us hope that will not happen. But I'm now convinced that your reputation is well deserved."

"I only wish," said the Saint frankly, "that I knew more about yours."

"It would depend entirely on who you heard it from. But I expect that is something we have in common."

The Saint looked out of the window.

"Where are we now? Isn't that the Stadt Park?"

"Yes. You know Vienna well, Simon?"

"Well enough. I know where to eat, sleep, and enjoy myself. That's all one need know about a town."

Max laughed.

"Especially the last. Perhaps we can trade some addresses. By the way, have you been to Baden?"

"Not often. I'm not old or rheumatic enough to need the spa waters, and the Casino is really pretty small time. Young Leopold's mother wouldn't be seen dead there, I'm sure, and the town strikes me as being a sort of undertaker's happy hunting ground. But why do you ask?"

"My place is near there," replied Annellatt, pressing his foot down on the accelerator as they came out on the main road to Schönbrun. "At this hour of the day it should not take us long to reach it."

For a while he devoted himself to thrusting the car along the broad avenue without further talk. As they passed Schönbrun Palace, the Saint wondered, as he always did when he saw that great edifice, about the composition of an Imperial mind which could think in terms of a summer cottage with a thousand rooms. They left the Palace behind them and headed south-west towards the Neusiedlersee, skirting the Wienerwald.

When they were in the country, Max really let the Mercedes go. It seemed to handle itself as if it had a spirit and a mind of its own. Max glanced at Simon.

"I love driving fast," he remarked. "Life is so slow. Anything which can speed it up and make it amusing is so much to the good."

Simon concurred, with a reservation.

"Almost anything. I can't stand roller coasters, or those other machines that spin you around in three or four directions at once. I'm afraid you'll never see me having a big time in the Prater."

"That is childish stuff, fit only for the Viennese who are all children at heart. That's what makes them so dangerous. They are loving, happy, and utterly ruthless, like children. You and I are adults. I think we understand each other, yes?"

"I might understand you better," said the Saint levelly, "if I really knew anything about you."

"I thought I had told you a lot, for such a short acquaintance."

"Not about yourself."

"Do I seem such a mysterious personage?"

"It's a bit of a mystery to me," said the Saint bluntly, "how a man who makes such mistakes as you have can be as successful as you've obviously been. Or expect to go on getting away with it."

"What mistakes, for instance?"

"For instance, assuming that the Gestapo wouldn't be wise to your back garage exit."

"I still think it was true at the time. I did not say they would never find it."

"But it was a bad under-estimate, all the same. Now, you were sure that the Malffy Palais wasn't being watched, at least tonight. Perhaps because they were waiting for Frankie at your flat. But they know you're involved in the Necklace business with her. The Rat used your name when he started to question me. So why wouldn't they know about this country place of yours? Why are you sure they're such an inefficient lot, this Viennese Gestapo?"

Max shrugged.

"The Austrians are not a very efficient race. But we do get things done all the same. You may remember the old joke in the War. 'The situation in Berlin is serious but not hopeless. The situation in Vienna is hopeless but not serious.' That really sums up our national character."

"But you lost the War."

"In a sense, yes. But we made a very good recovery. And when Hitler took over this year he did so because he wanted our gold reserves, which were amongst the highest in Europe —better, I believe, even than those of England."

The Saint did not reply for a long while. When he finally spoke it was thoughtfully.

"And still you haven't given me the answers. You just come out as a charming and delightful chap, and probably a thorough-going crook. Perhaps that's the real reason Frankie picked you as a colleague. You must have some useful contacts both in high places and in the underworld."

Max plucked a cigarette from a gold case, deftly performing the operation with one hand. Simon pulled out the car lighter and lit it for him. Annellatt's face appeared weary and almost sad in the brightening glow.

"You are right, of course. I have the entrée into many circles. But the story of my life is long and rather unhappy. I do not like to think about it myself, although admittedly it always lies in the back of my mind."

"All right," said the Saint indifferently. "Keep it to yourself then."

But Max ignored him. He kept his eyes fixed on the road ahead and had the aspect of someone utterly alone, lost in his own bitter memories.

"I was born in Tyrol, the son of a poor farmer. Tourists find that Alpine region very picturesque and beautiful, and they think its inhabitants always look happy and contented. So they do. But that is only to please the tourists!"

He changed gear to negotiate a hill.

"What visitors don't know is that many of the Tyrolese have an entirely subnormal level of existence. Indeed, the kindly tourist would be horrified if he knew the extent of poverty there. That is why it is kept from him, because the Tyrolese need his money, even though, to speak frankly, they don't much like tourists."

The car surged forward as he changed back into high.

"I'm not too keen on most tourists myself," Simon admitted. "Somehow, every country always seems to export its worst specimens. Or maybe going abroad brings out the worst in them."

"Yes, but you dislike them from the vantage point of superiority. You are rich and aristocratic. I can tell you it is not very pleasant to know that others are wealthy and wasting food when you and your family are poor and hungry. My mother died when I was ten of consumption, aggravated by malnutrition. No, let's be honest, starvation would be more accurate. The fact that she was regularly knocked about by my father, who was a drunken brute, did not help. But perhaps he only drank to forget how unable he was to cope with the miserable situation of his family."

Simon noticed that the knuckles of Max's hands showed white as he gripped the wheel with sudden intensity. Then, as if coming back from a long distance, he continued.

"We were a large family. Poor families often are, in this country at any rate. There were too many for my father to provide for. We had to fend for ourselves. Two of my sisters and a brother died, simply because they could not, how do you say it, make the grade. Another brother emigrated to the United States, where he has obviously done quite well, for though we have never heard from him since, I saw his name in the paper connected with a Grand Jury investigation in

New York." Max chuckled. "It was my brother who was being investigated."

His expression became sombre again.

"Two of my other sisters were forced to sell themselves to tourists who admired the beauties of Tyrol a little too personally. One of them now lives in Innsbruck and the other in St Anton. Both are married and run excellent pensions of extreme respectability." His irrepressible Austrian humour flashed back for an instant in his eyes. "They do not approve of me. I am the black sheep of the family."

The Saint was sympathetic to Max's story, but he was also aware that it was a pitch for his good will.

"You don't seem to have done so badly for yourself," he observed.

"I've done very well. I realised early that life is what you make it. I decided to make mine extremely comfortable. That I have done."

"I'm glad your story has a happy ending."

Max gave him a steady look. "That was not part of my bargain with life. I did not ask for happiness. People who are happy are either saints or idiots."

"Point taken," Simon conceded. "I'm happy!"

"Yes, you may be a 'Saint' but not quite the usual kind, and that naturally makes me want to ask questions of my own."

"Fire away," said the Saint. "It costs nothing to ask."

"I was wondering what brought you to Vienna, before you so providentially met Frankie."

The Saint sighed.

"Everyone seems to be curious about that," he said. "But I'm afraid that's one I'm not answering. Perhaps I'll tell you all about it in a couple of hundred years, and I think it might amuse you. But for now you'll have to take my word that it had absolutely nothing to do with you, Frankie, or the Hapsburg Necklace."

He knew now that Annellatt's reminiscence had also been a

bid for reciprocal confidence, but Max seemed to accept its failure with good grace.

"That at least is worth knowing," Annellatt said, and drove on in silence for several kilometres.

After some time he braked suddenly and swung the car off on to a side road, which joined the main one where two ruined castles flanked it on opposite sides. Simon had seen them before and knew that to get to them they must have by-passed the town of Baden. They were called Rauhenstein and Rauheneck, and they flanked the road to Mayerling. Simon figured they must have been built by two rival barons who wanted to be near enough to each other to have a good bash-up when they felt like it. It occurred to him that the Middle Ages must have been full of fun like that.

They travelled a short while down the lane, twisting and turning as the road took them. Then suddenly ahead of them loomed another castle, looking in the bright morning sunlight like something painted on the backdrop of an operetta. This one was not ruined and indeed seemed to be in excellent repair.

Max drove the car to the entrance gate which was guarded by two towers and blocked by heavy wooden doors.

"Here we are," he said, and blew a tattoo on his car horn.

In a moment or two the doors opened on silent, well-oiled hinges. Max drove the car through the gate and into a stone-flagged courtyard.

"Let me relieve at least one of your anxieties," he said. "This place, in the official records, is owned by a Baron von Birkehügel of Salzburg. I think it will take even the Gestapo a long time to discover that I have ennobled myself, and to identify him with me."

The Castle was of that typical Austrian kind in which Renaissance classical details had been added to plaster over a medieval stone framework. The walls, Simon judged, would probably be about six feet thick, but the effect of the Renaissance overlay was graceful, light, and charming. He turned to his host.

"Very nice. Just what everyone should have. When does the chorus come on?"

Max laughed and got out of the car. Simon followed suit. An elderly man hurried towards them from under the gateway arch. He was evidently a retainer of sorts for he was wearing a green baize apron.

"Good evening, Anton," said his master in German. "I have brought a friend with me, Mr Templar, an English gentleman. Please see that a room is prepared for him at once."

The old man bowed towards the Saint, bending almost double.

"Good morning, sir," he said in English. "Welcome to Schloss Duppelstein."

Simon returned his greeting and glanced around the courtyard before following him into the Castle, which consisted of a main central portion which obviously housed the state rooms, as indicated by a row of large windows overhung with carved pediments, and two wings, each fronted by an arcade, above which ran a roofed wooden gallery, carved in a fanciful manner and painted in gay colours. Above these rose plaster-covered walls and two tiers of windows. The battlements of the Castle had been removed in Renaissance days and the structure had been given a tile roof in the French style.

A figure came out on to the wooden gallery of the left wing. It was female, lovely, and Frankie.

III

How Leopold's car was borrowed, and
Herr Annellatt provisioned a picnic

1

The Saint slept until midday. Then he got up and had a long hot bath and a shave. Feeling much rested and quite peckish, he followed Anton who came to lead him to the dining-room.

The inside of the Castle betrayed its medieval origin, although the stone walls had been plastered over and slit windows replaced by wider ones. According to upper-class Austrian custom, wall spaces whenever possible were embellished with the skulls, horns, and antlers of slaughtered animals. The passion which aristocrats in all lands have for killing wild creatures in great numbers always struck the Saint as distasteful, although he had shot some big game himself when it had seemed adventurous. But whatever killing he did was very selective, and it would not have done to hang the heads of his victims on the walls of his home, since many of them were human.

Anton led him through an enormous drawing-room, furnished for the most part in Louis Quinze style, but containing some comfortable-looking sofas and armchairs as well.

He stopped for a moment by another door.

"May I point out to your lordship," he said in English, "that the central part of this house is wired with burglar alarms on this floor because of the great value of its contents.

One cannot go even from one of the state rooms into another without setting off an alarm in this part of the building." He cast his eyes to heaven. "Alas, it is necessary in these *schreckliche* modern days of danger and violence. In the old times before the War such a thing would never have been thought of."

"I take it," said the Saint, "that guests are expendable. I mean, the guest wing isn't wired, or is it?"

Anton shook his head.

"No, sir. There is nothing of great value there."

"I suppose that goes for me," murmured the Saint, as Anton opened the door to the dining-room for him.

Max, Frankie and Leopold were seated at the table and had already begun their meal. Thai was once again curled in his favourite position round his master's shoulders. It was a pleasant domestic scene of upper-crust life in Central Europe. But it had overtones which jarred slightly.

For one thing, Annellatt, suave and well-mannnered though he was, was not upper-crust. The Saint could not help but feel that the other two were only there because of Max's dubious respect for conventional ethics and procedures. Of course, that should not be held against them. Their partnership with Max was a purely pragmatic one. In the ordinary course of society life they and Max would have been in different orbits.

But there was more to it than that. The Saint felt almost as if he were looking at one of those drawings in magazine competitions which incorporate deliberate errors. There was something wrong with this picture, although he couldn't quite put his finger on what it was. Perhaps it was no more than the rather bizarre events which had brought them all together.

He decided that for the time being he was not going to let it bother him. He was hungry and in a cheerful mood.

"Ach, good morning, Simon," cried Annellatt, getting to his feet. "I trust you slept well?"

"Like the proverbial baby," said the Saint. "Except that real babies usually seem to wake up yowling." He tickled the Siamese cat behind the ears. "How did he get here—don't tell me he drove his own little car."

"Frankie brought him, in his travelling basket. I did not want to risk having to leave him at the flat in an emergency." Max pulled out a chair. "Please forgive us for having started lunch, but I did not want to hurry you."

The Saint smiled at Frankie as he took his seat.

He said: "I did have a nasty dream that I was kidnapped by the Gestapo. Most realistic it was."

"Max has told us about your unpleasant adventure," she said. "Really, Austria has become quite barbaric since the Germans took over."

Her voice was warm, and her concern seemed genuine and spontaneous.

Simon was struck anew by her unusual charm. He wondered how much of it was deliberate—or conversely, to what degree it was natural. One never knew with Austrians. Charm was a national characteristic which with them was both hereditary and cultivated. They used it delightfully—and quite ruthlessly.

Leopold, who had also risen to his feet, gave Simon a short stiff little bow and sat down again. As far as the Saint was concerned, the young Count's Austrian charm must have been sent to the cleaners. It certainly wasn't around, and hadn't been since they met.

Anton and a serious young footman called Erich waited on the table, and the conversation touched only on general topics. For some reason, the Saint took an instant dislike to Erich. He was at a loss to explain this to himself, for Erich was respectful, polite, and efficient, which is all that is really required of footmen. But there was something about the young man's carefully blank dark eyes, and the way his sandy hair and bleached eyebrows seemed to make his personality fade away, that made the Saint vaguely uneasy about him.

Coffee and liqueurs were served after lunch in the drawing-room, and when the servants had withdrawn, Herr Annellatt quickly got down to business.

"Now, about the Necklace," he announced briskly, "we must complete our plan."

Simon rotated his balloon glass gently, swirling its pale gold contents up the sides.

"I thought we already had a general plan," he said. "All it needs is a man of exceptional strength, agility and cunning, who can climb in and out of castles like a cat and fight his way out of trouble if necessary—or think his way out if needs be."

"In fact, someone like the Saint," Annellatt said. For a moment Simon thought he was actually purring, but then he realised it must be the cat.

"Since you don't seem to have anyone who fits the bill," Simon replied modestly.

The Count sprang to his feet.

"Mr Templar would be worse than useless," he blurted out angrily. "He is a foreigner and speaks no Hungarian. If anybody goes it should be me."

"I can't see that it makes any difference whether one speaks Hungarian or not," said the Saint. "If the breaker-in is discovered they'll merely shoot him out of hand or slap him in jail for the rest of his life. It won't do him any good to protest in his best Magyar that he's just a plumber who's forgotten his tools."

"So how do you plan to break into the Castle?" asked Frankie in her most adoring manner.

"Yes, how?" echoed Leopold, in a contrastingly scornful tone.

The Saint felt sorry for him. The young man was obviously in love with Frankie and was insanely jealous of her undisguised fascination with the Saint. Flattering though it was, it was a complication that Simon could have done without. But since it was inescapable, as some philosopher said about something similar, he might as well relax and enjoy it.

His smile was like a kiss in her direction. It was no ordeal for him to play her game in spite of recognising the innate ruthlessness of her character.

"The plumber routine might be a gambit, at that," he said. "But I'd rather save it for a defence. I've always preferred a head-on surprise attack to complicated plots which are liable to trip over their own webs."

"But this is not some farm cottage," retorted Leopold. "It is a castle, with modern improvements."

"And I'm an oldfashioned retired burglar," Simon replied amiably, "which is the last kind of person they'd expect to be having a go at their battlements." Max drew on his cigar.

"In Vienna, I showed you as much as I could," he said. "That agricultural drain will bring you close to the castle—"

"And Frankie may know something about its weaknesses from the inside. Like secret passages and what not."

The girl shook her head.

"We were never at Este very much. My father liked his castle in Bohemia better."

"I see," said the Saint. "What you might call an *embarras de châteaux*."

"I don't know any secret passages, and I was not brought up to look at it like a burglar," Frankie said, with a flash of hauteur. "I can show you where the wine cellars were, and from there one could make one's way quite easily to where the Necklace is hidden."

"Suppose Mr Templar did get in," said Max, "how would he get out again?"

"That would be quite easy. If he took a rope he could let himself down from almost any of the outside windows. He'd have to wait until it was dark, of course. But there are so many rooms that I don't think even the Gestapo can have occupied them all."

"Right," said the Saint. "If I took a rope, a sleeping bag, a picnic basket, and a good book, I could stay for a week if I liked the place." He turned to Annellatt. "I shall have to give you a shopping list."

Max nodded.

"*Natürlich.* Anything you need can be obtained."

"The rope isn't a bad idea," said the Saint seriously. "And a few tools. Also, some clothes. Dressed as we are now, any of us would attract attention, whatever we were doing. We need the sort of things that any local workman would wear."

"—or a peasant girl," Frankie put in.

"You are not going," Leopold insisted.

Frankie drew herself up.

"If anyone is going to fetch the Necklace, I shall have to be there. I am its Keeper, and only I know where it is."

"You and Mr Templar," said Max. "Don't forget you have told him."

Simon shook his head.

"She has told me nothing except that it's in the Castle."

For a moment Max looked disconcerted.

"Oh. I thought you said . . . ?" He looked at Frankie enquiringly.

"I only said I had told him where it was. By that I meant that it was in the Castle. I did not say *where* it was hidden."

"I see, said Max thoughtfully. "But is that wise? Let us pray that nothing ever happens to you. But if it did, someone else should know where to look for it."

Farnkie's expression was enigmatic.

"I will do what I think best."

"If you tell anyone, you will tell me!" exploded Leopold. "I am one of the family. Mr Templar is a stranger and a noted . . . er . . ."

"Scoundrel?" supplied the Saint affably. "But that's what makes me the man for the job. Now, as a professional scoundrel, I'm thinking of something a bit more difficult for Max's list. To go with the clothes, we should have suitable identity papers. I know that they're always possible to get, if you know where to get them. Do Max's connections extend to that?"

Annellatt pursed his lips.

"It could be arranged."

"Then while you're at it, it would be better still to have a second set, in totally different names, to fall back on if the first lot get blown and we find ourselves on the lam—should I translate that?"

Annellatt's brown eyes bubbled momentarily with the impish merriment to which they were disarmingly susceptible.

"For my sins, I have learned some of those expressions," he said, but made a colloquial German translation.

He turned back to Simon.

If one can be done, both can be done," he said. "Anton will take and develop the necessary pictures, at once. They could be ready tonight. But the papers will take a little longer. It may take two days."

"The Hapsburg Necklace has been around for quite a few years," said the Saint. "I expect it can hold out for a couple more days, if the moths don't get to it."

Max stood up.

"Then make your list, Simon, and you can rely on me to do my part. While I am busy, will you all please regard Schloss Duppelstein as your own home."

2

Simon Templar, as a natural sybarite, greatly enjoyed the next forty-eight hours. Schloss Duppelstein was run luxuriously. He had a sumptuously furnished bedroom, with a bathroom attached, in the east wing of the Castle overlooking the courtyard. Frankie and Leopold were housed in the west wing. Max's quarters were in the central section. What delighted the Saint most about his accommodation, however, was the beautiful porcelain stove which stood in the corner of his bedroom and filled it with heat. He considered such stoves to be works of art and regretted that in Austria they were getting rarer as more modern forms of heating took over.

There was only one small cloud on his horizon. Erich was seconded to be Simon's valet, and the Saint got the impression that his work entailed a bit more snooping and curiosity about the Saint's affairs and effects than was normally permissible. Still, he reckoned he could deal with Erich firmly enough should the need arise, and he was never one to let such small matters, or the opinions of servants (or anyone else, for that matter) bother him.

Cars and tennis courts were at the disposal of the guests, and the weather was still warm enough to allow hardy individuals a quick dip in the icy, highly ornamented outdoor swimming pool. There were many lovely walks and rides in the hills around the Castle, and Max Annellatt had his own stables, filled with thoroughbreds, which he frankly admitted he could not ride.

Max was kindness itself, and he personally drove Simon, together with Frankie and Leopold, to see some of the sights of the surrounding countryside. His cat came along on the expedition, and even when his master drove, Thai lay on his shoulders like a fur collar. Simon came to the conclusion that the Siamese was the only creature Max really loved, for he treated it with a tenderness he never showed to humans. When they drove into the flat Burgenland to see the tomb of Haydn at Eisenstadt in the extraordinary church built in the shape of a huge rock, but not *in* a huge rock, Thai wandered off and got lost, and Max was distraught until the cat was discovered in one of the sentry boxes of the nearby Esterhazy Palace. Max joked that as a member of the Siamese Royal Family, Thai had probably been looking for a sentry to salute him, or even for Prince Esterhazy himself.

The following morning, Max left early on his self-imposed errands. Either from tact or malice, he asked Leopold to go with him for company, which the young man could scarcely refuse. A little later, Frankie suggested to Simon that they go for a drive in Leopold's car.

"I don't think he'd like that," Simon demurred.

"Perhaps," she said carelessly. "But if I tell him it was my idea, he won't dare to say so."

They both enjoyed each other's company and recognised that they shared a certain cavalier attitude to life, and they found it very pleasant to be temporarily free of the jealousies of Leopold, and Max's somewhat overpowering hospitality. Although Patricia Holm was never far from his thoughts, it was very tempting to accept Frankie's open readiness for a flirtation. And he would have had no guilty feelings about Patricia, who had never tried to tie him any more than he tied her. He was more wary of feeling guilty about Frankie, who he felt might get in deeper than she intended, if he went too far with her game. For all her independence of spirit, the Saint figured, she was the sort of girl who would take a love affair seriously, and seriousness in such matters can lead to the sort of complications the Saint did not want at that stage of his career.

However, he had no compunction about taking advantage of her ardour to make another attempt to find out from her where the Hapsburg Necklace was hidden in Schloss Este. She was wickedly cagey and enjoyed teasing him with hints while at the same time never giving him a clue as to its whereabouts. She told him her father had told her mother where the Necklace was hidden as he lay dying from a heart attack. Her mother had given the secret to Frankie when the girl came of age. Frankie told Simon all this while they were driving through the Wienerwald in the midst of glorious autumn colours.

He finally changed the subject, to try something else.

"How did you meet up with Max?" he asked. "He's not your league at all."

"My what?"

"Your class. He's not *Erstegesellschaft*, or even *Zweite*. In fact, he's not *Gesellschaft* at all. He admits it himself. He's a self-made man, and he's made a pretty good job of it, but you know how snobby you Austrian aristocrats are."

"That's why we adore the British and the Americans. They are the only other people who assume that the entire world was made for them. The Germans think that even if it was made for someone else, they can conquer it. The French think that France was made for them and the rest of the world doesn't count. The Italians say 'See Naples and die' or 'See Rome and pay.' They are not even a nation. And so it goes. But the English and Austrian upper classes seem to have sprung from the same womb."

"But not from the same father. Funnily enough I've heard exactly the same piece from some of my other Austrian friends. Do they teach it to you in school?"

For a moment Frankie looked annoyed. Then she burst out laughing.

"Certainly only the English-speakers can be as rude as the Austrians," she said. "But seriously, we are not nearly so snobby as we used to be. Nowadays we are quite democratic. We mix with all sorts of people." She gave Simon a mischievous look. "Especially if they have money."

"Well, Max certainly has that."

"Yes, he does. He's very well-known in business indeed in many other circles. I met him at a party given by an Archduke—a very poor Russian archduke."

"And you liked him straight off?"

She shrugged.

"One can like anyone one needs if one puts one's mine to it."

"I don't think you're as cynical as you pretend," Simon said.

"I'm not cynical at all. I'm just a realist. I needed someone like him, powerful and unscrupulous, with the power and influence money brings to help me get the Necklace back. I also knew that he is a strong Royalist. He would like to see the Pretender, young Archduke Otto, back on the throne. He told me himself that he was prepared to use all his power and money in the cause of the Monarchy. And that means that he must be in favour of the aristocracy." She made a sweeping gesture with her hand. "But he is the type who never does anything which he does not consider an investment."

"And so you told him about the Hapsburg Necklace?"

"Yes, but not where it is hidden." She gave him a sideways look. "I shan't even tell *you* that."

"How am I supposed to get it for you then? Just play Hunt the Necklace all over Schloss Este and hope I'll come across it?"

"No," she replied calmly. "You are taking me with you."

The Saint shook his head.

"So you've said before. But I'm not, you know. I always travel light. I never take any excess baggage if I can help it."

Her eyes laughed back at him. "*Touché*, but we'll see who wins, you or me. I might try by myself. Then, if I fail, I can always fall back on you."

"You can fall back on me anytime, darling." replied the Saint gallantly. "But what has Max done for you so far?"

"He has put his organisation at my disposal, and found out things about the surroundings of Schloss Este that even I did not know. Even now, he is getting us false papers, which I would never know how to get. And he has men who would commit any crime that is necessary, at his orders—or for his money."

"What does he think he will get out of it, or shouldn't one ask?"

"When the Monarchy is restored he will be made a real baron. I shall see to it."

The Saint shrugged.

"I suppose that makes it all worth while."

"Of course. His grandchildren will even be accepted into the aristocracy."

"If he ever gets around to having any. But you mean he himself wouldn't be accepted?"

"Certainly not. He is a tradesman by birth."

"I see. When is a baron not a baron? When he isn't two generations removed from vulgar trade. And how did Leopold get in on the act?"

"Because he is my second cousin, and I have known him since childhood and can trust him completely. That is something worthwhile."

"Yes, definitely. He belongs all right. But whether or not that fact makes him a good Necklace-getter-backer is something else."

"He is young and foolish sometimes, but he is not a fool. He is also a noted shot."

"That might certainly come in handy," said the Saint. "Actually, he seems a nice enough lad, even though I don't think he's crazy about me. Of course, he's in love with you, as you well know."

Frankie sighed dramatically.

"Ach, it is such a nuisance. But men can get so silly!"

"Sometimes it's fun to be silly," said the Saint.

She looked at him provocatively from beneath her long lashes. "Are you ever silly, Simon?"

This was the edge of the thin ice that he still hoped to skate around.

He shook his head.

"Never. I often lose my heart, but never my head."

He blew her a kiss with the tips of his fingers. She caught it, pressed it to her lips and blew him one back. The Saint pretended to catch it and put it in his pocket.

"I'll keep it for bedtime," he said. "It'll go well with my Ovaltine."

It was a happy excursion, and they were as far removed from the realities of Nazi-occupied Austria as was Johann Strauss—and indeed most of the Austrians at that time.

When they got back to Schloss Duppelstein late in the afternoon, they were met by Leopold who informed them stiffly that Max was waiting to show them the stables.

"*Furchtbar!*" exclaimed Frankie. "I quite forgot to tell you, Simon. He wants to show us his prize stallion. It is called Neville Chamberlain because it's by Aeroplane out of Munich. You see it is a joke."

"It might have been more suitable to call him Lloyd George," Simon remarked.

"Lloyd George? What did he have to do with Munich?"

"Nothing at all," said the Saint, "but he was much more the stallion type."

She shook her head in puzzlement.

"I do not understand. You too are making a joke, yes?"

"You're too young to explain it to," Simon told her. "But come along." He pointed to where Leopold was already striding in the direction of the stables. "He'll be your second cousin once removed if he has a stroke."

Max Annellatt was watching the stallion being led around a tanbark ring by a stable-boy.

"I shall have the papers after lunch tomorrow," he said. "Also the clothes you wanted—it was easy to buy them but now they are being made to look not so clean and new. My horse is beautiful isn't he?"

"He is indeed," Simon said unreservedly.

"Tomorrow morning you must take him for a ride."

"If Frankie will go with me."

"I will kill you if you try to leave me behind," she said.

Leopold scowled, but for once made no protest, and Simon wondered if Max had been giving him some avuncular advice about how not to cope with a young woman's provocation to the rivalries of courtship.

In spite of the boy's sulkiness and juvenile jealousies, he liked Leopold and felt considerable sympathy for him. After all, the young man was up against the ruthlessness of womankind and in particular the ruthlessness of Frankie, who, Simon judged, combined the self-centredness of aristocracy with a singleness of purpose which in itself did not allow much room for the consideration of others. Whatever Frankie wanted to do, she did; whatever she wanted to get, she got. It was not that she lacked feeling, but she used people for her own purposes and indeed considered that most people had been created to be used by her.

She was certainly, by her own admission, using Max; but Simon suspected that the reverse was also true. Certainly Annellatt was no fool, and in his way he was certainly as ruthless as Frankie. If it came to a clash of wills and ambitions, Simon wondered which one would win. It might be amusing to find out.

The following afternoon, to Simon's surprise, Leopold asked him if he would like to do a little *Auerhahn* shooting. The invitation was gruffly tendered, but Simon understood that he was making an effort to be pleasant. After all, except for his unfounded jealousy, there was no reason for him to dislike Simon. The Saint accepted because he wanted to find out more about Leopold's character, not because he wanted to shoot *Auerhahn*, a sport he particularly disapproved of because of the peculiar and particular way it was done. The birds could only be shot when they were singing their love songs, at which time the males perched in the branches of trees and sang with their eyes closed. Simon had always thought it was really not quite cricket to sneak up on a lover thus engaged and do him in. After all, he would be seriously annoyed himself if someone tried such a dirty trick on him. Not that he ever sang with his eyes closed, or even open for that matter, while he was making love.

They didn't get any *Auerhahn*. Simon had guessed that they wouldn't, and that the invitation had merely been a friendly overture, because the birds mate in the spring and not in the autumn. Nevertheless, they had a pleasant walk in the woods and Leopold turned out to be a surprisingly amusing companion when he was not being tormented by his love for Frankie. At one point he even entertained Simon with a hilarious imitation of Max talking to Thai.

It was dusk when they returned to the Schloss. They found Annellatt and Anton in the State Drawing-room. It was immediately apparent that something was wrong from the expressions on their faces.

"Thank God you are back," groaned Max. "The worst has happened!"

"Hitler and Stalin have been jointly awarded the Nobel Peace Prize," suggested the Saint; but his flippancy was brittle and unsmiling.

Annellatt waved his hands wildly.

"This is serious, Simon. Frankie has gone!"

3

Leopold stopped as if he had been struck. His face was deathly pale.

"What do you mean?" he demanded hoarsely.

Max was more agitated than Simon would have thought possible. His hand shook as he put it up to his forehead, and the whites of his eyes showed like those of a nervous horse.

"She took the clothes I had brought, to try on, and the papers to go with them. And just now, Anton found this note in the hall."

It was significant that he thrust the paper towards Simon and not Leopold.

The Saint took it. It was short and to the point and said in German:

Dear Friends,

Do not be annoyed with me. I have a plan of my own for getting the Necklace. It is better that I carry it out alone. But if I am not back in three days' time, come and get me out of Schloss Este. I am sure Simon can do it even if it's impossible!

Love to you all and Thai.
Frankie.

The Saint felt that old surge of tingling excitement, the herald of adventure to come.

"Perhaps we can still head her off," babbled Leopold.

"And risk fouling up this plan of hers for getting the Necklace—whatever it is?"

"Who cares about the Necklace?" Leopold ranted. "It is only Frankie who matters."

Max was lighting a cigarette. It was a gold-tipped Russian one, and its most oriental fragrance, though it evidently pleased him, irritated Simon's nostrils. In spite of his trembling fingers, Max's voice was firm and decisive.

"It so happens that Frankie cares a lot about the Necklace. So much that she is willing to risk her life for it. We owe it to her to give her a chance with her plan, whatever it costs her. It would only be tragic if we could not complete the plan, if she fails."

Simon gave him a quizzical look. This combination of practicality and romantic idealism was very Austrian. It was just the sort of thing which had caused the downfall of their great Empire. No man can serve two masters, and the Austrians always tried to please everyone with the result that their priorities often got hopelessly muddled. But he didn't think Max's were.

"Unfortunately," Simon reminded him, "none of us has the faintest idea where to look for the Necklace. We can only hope that she does get her hands on it."

"And so you would just leave her to do everything alone," accused Leopold, ready to work himself up into one of his quick rages.

"Calm yourself, Leopold." Max spoke authoritatively. "I am sure that Simon is thinking of something more than that."

"I'm thinking that at least we know where she's headed for," said the Saint. "And if it's too late to stop her, at least we could be a lot closer than this if she needs help. How far is it to Schloss Este?"

"About an hour's drive. It's on the border, as a matter of fact."

Simon looked thoughtful.

"I'd rather avoid the official frontier check-point. That would get us involved with passports, visas, and all the other red tape of customs and immigration."

Max nodded vigorous agreement.

"Especially since the Germans who have occupied the Castle, the Gestapo, have turned the whole village of Este into a *verboten* area since they made the Schloss their headquarters for both Hungary and Austria."

"How do you know that?"

"I know a lot of things. It is my business to find out as much of what is going on everywhere as possible."

"Why did they pick Schloss Este?"

"Because it is large, and because of its situation. With the river on one side and their gun emplacements on the others, barbed wire, mine fields and all the rest, there is no way in unless one is officially welcomed." Max grimaced. "And that is not a welcome many people would like."

"I wonder how Frankie thinks she can get in."

Max spread his hands apart, palms upward.

"Who knows? She may have thought of some story to go with her peasant clothes, but what good that would do I cannot think."

The Saint concurred in that admission with a slight tightening of his lips, but he forced himself to keep thinking constructively.

"She may have thought of using that drain that you were telling us about in Vienna," he said. "But whether she did or not, it still seems to be the likeliest way in for us. The frontier follows the river there, doesn't it?"

"Yes."

"Then that's where we'll cross to Schloss Este—the shortest way."

Annellatt pondered for only a few seconds, puffing jerkily at his acrid cigarette.

"The only way," he agreed. "But someone must stay here to be in charge in case anything goes wrong. That will be you, Leopold. Simon and I will go together." He drew himself up theatrically. "If that is the end of us, you must carry on."

"No," said Leopold firmly and with unexpected authority. "It is I who must go. Frankie is my cousin and the Necklace is to do with my family." He gave Max's pudgy form a cruelly critical survey. "Besides, you are too old—or at any rate, not in condition."

Max had had his moment, and it might have been uncharitable to suspect that he was relieved rather than affronted by its rather tactless rejection.

"Perhaps you are right," he sighed, but could not resist getting in a return dig: "And besides, there should be someone left with the brains to cope with emergencies and to organise another attempt if necessary. You and Simon will go. I reluctantly will remain behind."

He bowed gracefully to the Saint, who bowed back.

"Very sensible," Simon remarked. "Valour is the better part of idiocy. Only fools get medals. The bright boys get made generals by being able to read maps at Headquarters Command."

In less than an hour, Max had the whole expedition organised, and they were on their way to the border in Max's Mercedes, followed by Anton, Erich, and another man in a large Opel saloon. When Max was not being Austrian and scatty he could act with positively Teutonic efficiency. That was probably how he had become a millionaire in a country where most people are too lackadaiscial to be ambitious, or at any rate to fulfill what ambitions they do have.

The Saint and Leopold were dressed as workmen and had papers identifying them as "agricultural engineers"—a magnificently sesquipedalian title in German that Max had dreamed up for the delectation of a bureaucratic mentality fascinated by high-sounding designations, which would cover almost any simulated activity from map-making to testing electric mains. That might not help them much if they were caught inside Schloss Este itself, but they would have to tackle that eventuality if and when it came.

It was a warm night for October. What was more important, however, was that it was a moonless one because it was overcast. Max gave them more information as he drove.

"The river is a tributary to the Dekes, which runs into the Raba, which flows along the border."

"Then it is not a very wide river," Leopold said.

"But a swift one, and that is what we need. Speed is essential, as you will be in a rowing boat travelling downstream. The less time you are in the open the less danger you will run."

"The boat is to be supplied by you, I take it," said the Saint.

"Exactly. I keep one there—for fishing! You will drift silently down river and steer across it. I and my men will create a diversion farther upstream, while you become sewer rats. I am sewer you will do well—that is an English-type, joke, no?"

"And you'll be our Pied Piper. That is an Austrian-type joke, yes?"

"Yes," agreed Max enthusiastically.

"Austrian corn can be as green as English corn," said the Saint philosophically.

Max looked baffled, but then he laughed heartily.

"I am glad we understand each other's jokes, my friend. We are much the same, you and I. If you will forgive another English-type joke, we can wave to each other from the same length."

It was Simon's turn to be momentarily baffled.

"As Ma Coni said to Pa Coni," he quipped weakly, and winced as he said it.

"I think you two have gone mad," interrupted Leopold.

"You are just talking nonsense. How do we get back with no boat?"

Max looked at him out of the corners of his eyes.

"That is up to you. I suggest you may swim. It will be a bit chilly, but it will only be a short trip. A little way downstream you will see an electricity pylon. Near it is my wooden hut. I will have someone stationed in it, with a change of clothes for you both, and for Frankie, we hope."

"I hope you get the sizes right," said Simon. "My tailor is awfully particular about what I wear."

"Here we are," Annellatt said at last, manoeuvring the car off the road and into a thicket.

He switched off its engine and its lights. A moment later the second car joined them and did the same, and Anton and his two helpers alighted and were dismissed by Annellatt with a gesture, as if they already had their instructions.

Max led Simon and Leopold along a narrow path through the trees towards the sound of moving water which was like a Wagnerian overture. The thunder of the rushing stream became louder with each step they took, and suddenly they came out upon the riverbank and the water swirled in silver whorls at their feet, seeming to have a luminescence of its own.

A boat was tied to a stake on the bank, straining as if it was eager to be off. The Saint and Leopold each had a workman's satchel containing the tools Simon had asked for, also a flashlight, a long knife and a compass. Each of them had a Walther PPK .32 calibre pistol in a shoulder holster. Max carried an old Gladstone bag that held sausage, bread, cheese, and two bottles, which he put in the boat. The Saint considered that some of those provisions were unnecessary and a bit bulky for carrying, especially up drains, but Max had been so enthusiastic about his preparations that Simon had not wanted to hurt his feelings.

Leopold got into the boat, and Simon followed him and

took up the oars. Max untied the craft and pushed it into the stream where it was immediately taken by the current.

At that moment there was a sudden rattle of firecrackers up the river where Max's henchmen were starting their diversionary tactic. A series of incandescent balls floated up, suffusing the sky in that direction with a multi-coloured glow.

"Goodbye," called Max in a low voice, "and good luck, my friends. You will need it."

Then his figure was lost in darkness as the boat surged into the middle of the stream.

Simon pulled hard on the oars, forcing the craft diagonally across the river. A searchlight flashed out from the Castle fortifications above, stabbing towards the point where Max's men were putting on their firework display, well hidden in the underbrush. It looked as if Annellatt's plan had worked, and the Saint and Leopold would be able to make it safely to the opposite bank.

Then suddenly, the searchlight began to swing in their direction, its operator apparently not being satisfied that he was getting the whole picture. The brilliant sword-like beam played along the opposite bank of the river, lighting up the stream as it went as well. It would only be a matter of seconds before it discovered the boat.

Then, all at once, it stopped dead in its swinging arc. Max was standing full in its beam, waving gaily in the direction of the Castle ramparts.

Simon understood at once what Max was up to. If the Austrian could hold the searchlight long enough, the boat would gain its haven. There was a crunch as its keel grounded on the opposite bank. Simon and Leopold leapt ashore and shoved the boat back into the current where it was immediately swept away. They then ran, doubled, for the drain.

The last thing Simon saw as he and Leopold slid into the opening was the debonair figure of Max. At any moment he might as likely as not have been rewarded with a bullet, but no shot came. Max gave a final wave and walked in a leisurely fashion into the shadows. It was a typically Austrian gesture, gallant, heroic and idiotic. But he had saved their skins for the time being.

4

Simon and Leopold crawled up the drain. Their progress was slow because they had to go on all fours and were encumbered with what they had to carry. Also the floor was covered with pools of filthy water and slippery silted mud.

The Saint led the way, his flashlight probing ahead along concrete walls covered with green scum stretching away into the darkness. Behind him Leopold scrabbled, panted and occasionally swore.

"Never mind, laddie," the Saint encouraged him. "Think of the poor midgets who have to tunnel the holes in Gruyère."

Finally they came upon a small dome in the roof of the tunnel. In it was what appeared to be the manhole Max had mentioned. Rising on his knees with some difficulty in that cramped space, the Saint shoved at its lid. It did not budge. Bracing himself, he asserted the full force of his great strength, and when the Saint did that most things budged or got moved around in some way. The manhole lid was no exception, and once it had been loosened from its rusty moorings the Saint was able to push it aside quite easily, even though there appeared to be something heavy resting on top of it. He climbed through the aperture cautiously and noiselessly.

All was dark, almost unnaturally so. The Saint waited for a moment, listening for some noise which might indicate what part of the Castle's grounds he had come up in, and also whether anyone had heard or observed his arrival on the scene.

Nothing stirred, and in the impenetrable dark the Saint felt secure enough to risk moving around. Almost immediately he

ran into something hard with a sharp edge. It seemed to be a
large box. Feeling his way around it the Saint encountered a
wooden wall. He was evidently in some sort of shed, and he
decided therefore that it would be all right to have a quick
look around with his torch.

His flashlight showed him immediately why the manhole
had remained undiscovered by the recently arrived Germans.
It was indeed in a shed, and had been covered by the heavy
wooden box which the Saint's shin and probing fingers had
just encountered. The box was stencilled GEHEIMWEIT
GESELLSCHAFT. LÜBECK. HOLSTEIN., and it had once probably
contained farming implements or something of that order, for
the shed was evidently used as an agricultural storage place,
judging by the spades, forks and other farm tools which leant
against its walls. The box had obviously, perhaps fortuitously,
been placed on top of the manhole, which explained why the
Germans had not found the latter and also why the Saint had
had some extra difficulty in moving the lid.

The Saint called to Leopold to come up through the aperture and lend him a helping hand. When the other stood
panting beside him, Simon made a sweeping invitation with
the flashlight.

"Make yourself at home, chum. It's not exactly the Ritz,
but it's so difficult to get the right sort of staff these days."

He stood his torch on the wooden crate, opened the Gladstone bag beside it, and began to take out the provisions.

"What is that for?" Leopold demanded.

"Dinner," said the Saint succinctly. "An army marches on
its stomach, as Napoleon was always telling me."

"But we have not the time to waste—"

"We can't find a way into the Schloss in the dark. And we
can't creep around looking for one with flashlights, unless we
want someone to hose us down with a machine gun. And
even if we were only challenged, I don't think we could con-
vince anyone that agricultural engineers work at night. We'll
have to wait for the crack of dawn." Simon was cutting slices

of bread and capping them with slices of sausage, and he proffered one to Leopold on the point of his knife. "Meanwhile, this'll be something less to lug around."

They had a surprisingly pleasant meal and were hungry enough for the liverwurst, cheese and hunks of bread to taste like food fit for kings—or at any rate monarchs on the run. They drank most of the wine, and to his delight the Saint discovered that the label on the other bottle declared it to contain Delamain cognac. "Nothing but the best," murmured the Saint appreciatively, and poured them each a noggin in the glasses which Max had not forgotten to pack, but had thriftily not chosen from his finest crystal.

After which, he took the Gladstone bag for a pillow and stretched himself out as comfortably as he could on the bare floor.

"Switch off the chandelier when you settle down, and save the electricity bill," he said, and closed the eyes.

Even after the light went out Leopold could be heard moving restlessly and unhappily, until the Saint, with his amazing capability of controlled relaxation, drifted away into peaceful slumber.

The built-in alarm clock which was another of the Saint's mental gifts awakened him within what his luminous watch hands told him was only minutes of the hour for which he had set it. The hut was still dark, but there was just enough light outside to limn the crack underneath the rickety door.

He was cold and stiff but quite pleased with life. This was the sort of expedition which compensated for the boring interludes when there was no excitement, no danger, and no fun and games. That such dull periods were not all that frequent, nor of great duration, in the Saint's life, made no difference. They did come along occasionally and that was too often as far as he was concerned.

He roused the snoring Leopold, who must have dropped off eventually, if only from exhaustion and the wine and brandy, and the young man sat up in sudden alarm. "Wo *sind* Wir?" he gasped, his eyes still glazed with sleep.

"The Hotel Sacher," Simon replied cheerily, and handed Leopold a staling crust. "Room service coming up."

They made a swift meal of the rest of the sausage and cheese and wine, discarding the glasses and the empty wine bottle along with the bag in which they had been carried; but the Saint stowed the remaining brandy in his workman's satchel. Delamain '14 was too good to chuck away. Then he opened the door of the shed cautiously.

Staying well in the shadows, they both peered out into the new day.

The sight which met their eyes would have been well suited to a travel poster. Two ridges of low tree-clad hills converged. Between them lay a small valley where nestled the hamlet of Este, which consisted of a few high-gabled cottages clustering around a large baroque church with an onion-shaped spire.

The village, however, was not what held their attention. Above it, set on a sheer stone cliff and perched like an eagle on its nesting place, was the Castle.

Even under such tense circumstances, Simon appreciated its beauty. The towering façade, shining white plaster on massive stone walls, rose storey upon storey. It was surmounted by a red-tiled roof, and behind this the immense medieval keep tower loomed, its battlements gnashing at the sky.

But not being tourists, they could not linger just to appreciate the view. They had to get up to that castle without being seen, and, what was more, they had somehow to get into it. Looking at its vast unwelcoming frontage, this last enterprise would have disheartened most men. That two unwanted strangers could penetrate such an imposing stronghold would have struck the average surveyor as a frivolous pipedream. But Simon Templar was not average in the least degree, and his whole life was dedicated to making just such fantasies come true.

Motioning Leopold to follow him, he made off quickly

across the area of small vegetable garden allotments in which
their overnight shelter was one of a number of similar sheds.
The villagers of Este evidently practised some form of com-
munal farming in the small amount of arable land available.
This often occurred in the hinterlands of Central Europe,
especially when the land was owned by a single landlord and
rented out to tenant farmers. The Saint judged that there was
no danger of minefields so far away from the surrounding
barbed wire perimeter defences, and he only hoped that whatever sentries were on duty there at that hour would be looking
outwards from the enclave and not inwards. He headed for
the left-hand hills rather than the right, for up against the latter was a huddle of new-looking wooden huts which probably
housed part of the military garrison.

It was only a matter of minutes before they had reached
the shelter of the woods, and they then set their course towards the Castle. The going was easy, for on the continent of
Europe forests are an industry and are kept clear of un-
dergrowth.

The sun was now well up and was beginning to warm even
the inner regions of the woods. A few late butterflies danced
madly amid bracken as if they knew they were performing a
last waltz before winter and death overtook them, and warm
woody scents began to fill the air.

Their passage, though easy, was slowed down by the fact
that they had to try not to be seen. But even so, it was not
long before they came to an opening in the trees where some
time ago the face of a cliff had fallen down the side of the
hill. The jagged rocks of this fall presented quite an obstacle.
For one thing they were steeply stacked, jumbled and in some
cases as jagged as dragon's teeth. For another they were
clearly visible from the entire valley below and especially
from the road which ran along the foot of the rock fall and up
to the Castle gate.

This hazard would have to be crossed as quickly as possible
and they would have to trust to luck that no one saw them

from the valley or came along the road while the traverse was being made.

Simon moved out into the open with Leopold following. The young man seemed at last to have tacitly accepted the Saint's leadership, or at least recognised his superior competence in this kind of activity. They squirmed Indian-fashion between the rocks on their bellies, only rising when a particularly large obstacle forced them to. The farther they got out into the open the more they could see of the road and conversely the more chance there was of their being spotted.

Suddenly a hoarse shout of command made them both duck down behind a large rock. Peeping cautiously around it they saw a small detachment of German soldiers marching up the road towards the Castle.

The Saint was surprised. Hungary, though sympathetically inclined towards Hitler's regime, was not then officially in the German orbit, and Admiral Horthy still managed to preserve autocratic rule in his own country. It must have gone against his grain and the feelings of many of his colleagues to be forced to allow the Gestapo to take over Schloss Este. And these German troops implied much more. Max was obviously right. The Castle was garrisoned by the *Wehrmacht*. That was going to make entry even more difficult.

Then Simon saw that the troops were guarding a prisoner, who walked along proudly, head up, in their midst. Leopold saw too, and gave an involuntary gasp. The Saint stilled him with a gesture.

The prisoner was Frankie.

IV

How Simon Templar changed costume, and a Reichsmarshal was deprived of tranports

1

Frankie marched along briskly, looking every inch the aristo-crat in spite of the peasant costume she wore. She had dropped the scarf from her head, and her raven hair glistened in the sun like a black plume. Then she and her guards vanished around a bend in the road.

Leopold was white-faced and shaking.

"They have captured her!" he whispered hoarsely.

"Could be," agreed the Saint. "On the other hand, it's her easiest way into the Castle."

"What do you mean?"

"Simply, that if you arrive at the village of Este, or even at the gates of the compound, and let it be known that you are the Countess Malffy and the real owner of the Castle, the guards are bound to pay attention to you. They'd be neglect-ing their duty if they failed to take you up to the Comman-dant for questioning."

"You mean, she did it on purpose?"

The Saint nodded.

"Knowing your cousin, it's on the cards. She's clever enough and daring enough—I'd almost say mad enough—to think it up and perhaps even get away with it."

"But she is captured. No one can save her now. They know

she has the secret of the Necklace, and the Gestapo stop at nothing."

"Since she thought this up, she must have a plan to save herself," said the Saint optimistically. "That is, after she's got the Necklace."

"I'm going to rescue her," declared Leopold, struggling to his feet.

Simon pulled him down again.

"It won't help if somebody sees you. Anyway, you can't take on a whole squad of soldiers single-handed."

The young man was almost beside himself with emotion.

"What better way to die?"

"As somebody once remarked," Simon said patiently, "the only trouble with death is that it is a permanent occupation. Wouldn't you be more useful alive?"

"Not so long as Frankie is in danger," replied Leopold, somewhat obscurely.

"I don't think she's in any actual danger at the moment. If I were the Commandant I'd find out what the higher-ups wanted me to do, and in German bureaucracy that means that the higher-ups will want to find out what *their* superiors think, and so on and so forth. That sort of thing takes time."

His words struck home.

"You are right," Leopold agreed. "But what can we do?"

"Well, to begin with, we can try to let Frankie know that we're around."

"I know." Leopold's eyes lit up. "I'll go back to the village. She must have friends there. Someone will be able to get a message to her."

"Not on your nelly you won't. They'd get a message straight to the Commandant. If that village doesn't have its quota of collaborators, I'm a bishop."

"What can we do then?"

The Saint stretched himself like a great lithe animal, but keeping well down behind the rock.

"You wait here. I'll go and recce."

"But what if you are captured?"

The Saint grinned.

"If I'm not back in three weeks, send a St Bernard with a cask of brandy after me, and don't forget it's got to be a 1914 Delamain."

"You make a joke of everything!" Leopold said petulantly. "You seem to forget that my cousin is in danger of being killed—or worse."

Simon put a hand on his shoulder.

"Don't worry, laddie, just because I try to see the lighter side of something doesn't mean I don't take it seriously. Now you wait back in the woods. Try not to expose yourself, as the bishop said to the actress. If I'm not back by nightfall, try to go back the way we came—swim across the river—and tell Max. He'll figure out what to do. He's got a vested interest in this business, aside from liking Frankie."

"Why can't I come with you?"

"Because someone's got to be sure to be able to take the bad news to Max." The Saint was swiftly transferring everything he considered unessential from his satchel to Leopold's, concluding with the cognac bottle. "Look after this for me, will you? And no dipping into it until I get back. We may need it to celebrate."

Then he turned and began climbing nimbly over the rocks in the direction of the Castle. He gained the woods on the other side of the cliff fall and turned to check on Leopold. The other waved to him rather forlornly.

Simon waved back, a buoyantly swashbuckling salute that conveyed its message of invincible confidence as eloquently as any words, and melted into the trees.

It was not long before he came out on a bluff overlooking the Castle. On this side it looked much more vulnerable to an attacking force, especially as the main entrance was here. A lone sentry paced back and forth across the open gate.

The Saint thought things over. The part of the Schloss he now overlooked was relatively low compared to the other opposite side which overhung the cliff. Here it was only three storeys high, except for the main keep tower rising from the centre of the edifice. Simon considered the possibility of climbing up to one of the windows overlooking the driveway to the main entrance. The snag, of course, was that he could easily be seen, and would in all likelihood anyway be spotted by the guard at the gateway if he made such an attempt. The Saint was always ready to take chances, but not the kind which would almost inevitably end in disaster.

There was nothing for it, he decided, but to work his way around in the edge of the woods on the bluff overlooking the Castle and see if one of the other sides did not offer a better prospect. He set off accordingly, keeping as far as possible out of sight, and assuming the plodding gait of a labourer going stolidly about some lawful business.

He soon found himself looking at an almost blank stone wall. On this side the Castle rose only two storeys from the ground because the bluff on which he stood ran right up to the Castle wall. As the Saint figured it, because of the sloping terrain on which the Castle stood, the inside of the building must consist of rooms on many different levels, and on the other side of the Castle there would be several floors below the point on which he stood.

The Saint stood back in the shade of the trees and took stock of the situation. Two windows overlooked his position, one above the other, but they were high up, and the sheer wall could only have been climbed with pitons.

Then his eye alighted on another potential method of getting into the Castle, which would not entail so many hazards as trying to scale the wall.

This was a basement window, half sunk into the ground. As Simon judged it, though small, it was still too large to be a dungeon light and probably led into one of the floors of the Castle which, because of the slope of the hill, would not necessarily be a basement on the other side. But good things usually have a snag, and in this case the catch was that the window was bisected by an iron bar. Nevertheless, the set-up looked promising, and he decided to investigate it more closely.

He took a deep breath, and sprinted across the intervening ground like a hunting panther. The distance was about forty yards, and he must have covered it in less than four seconds, veering at the end to roll prone into the narrow stone trough surrounding the window. Once there, he could only have been seen through the window itself, or from directly overhead: therefore if only nobody had been looking in exactly the right direction during those four fateful seconds, he would have got away with it.

After two or three breathless spine-tingling minutes, he ventured to believe that his luck might have held that long.

He peered through the window into what was obviously a storage room because it was filled with crates and boxes packed in an orderly fashion. It probably had been a storage place for some years and the window bar had been placed there not to keep anyone in but to keep intruders out.

The windowpane was an impediment for only as long as it took him to dig out the brittle putty which held it in its frame. The glass came out quietly, in one piece. Then he had plenty of room to work on the iron bar. It was thick and solidly set in stone, but its outer scale of rust was no tougher than a bride's first cake, and the core of ancient iron was no match for a modern hacksaw blade, which cut it almost as easily as hardwood.

Even with liberal applications of oil, however, the sawing could not be completely noiseless, and the tension of waiting for someone to hear it and come to investigate it stretched every second of the time it took into what felt like an hour.

The instant his last saw stroke freed the bar, Simon squirmed through the opening and dropped on to a packing case below the window.

Before taking another step, he replaced the iron bar where he had cut it from, fixing it in position with a couple of wedges of black insulating tape. From quite a short distance, the repair would be invisible enough to deceive anyone who gave it a casual inspection from outside.

Only then did he feel free to boost himself down off the crate and review his immediate surroundings in more detail.

He found himself in a large room with whitewashed walls. Opposite the window was the door. It was shut. He walked over and tried the latch. It worked smoothly. But no amount of tugging would open the door. It was obviously locked on the other side.

The Saint studied it thoughtfully. That it would open inwards towards him was indicated by its hinges which were on his side of the door. Therefore, to even a first-term student of housebreaking, it might almost as well have been unlocked. Of course, the naïve souls who were relying on the lock might not have been concerned with its vulnerability from the inside . . .

With the aid of pliers and the leverage of a screwdriver from his kit, Simon simply extracted the pins from the hinges. Luckily they were in good working condition and unrusted. It was then easy to prise the door out of its frame from that side, letting the lock itself serve as a clumsy but not irresistibly recalcitrant hinge.

He walked through the opening, and for the sake of appearances pulled the door back as near shut as possible behind him.

He was now in a passage leading off to his left and ending in a window which probably looked out over the cliff on the south side of the Castle and across the valley. Across from him were three doors. Two of them were small and looked as if they might lead into other storerooms. The one by the window, however, was larger and more imposing. The Saint decided that this one probably provided a route from the storeroom into the main body of the Castle. He walked up to it and stood for a moment listening. The only sound he could hear was a puzzling one. It was like the noise made by a buzzsaw with some of its teeth missing. At any rate, it did not sound human. The Saint tried the handle of the door, which then opened easily away from him. Swiftly the Saint slipped through.

The room on the other side looked as if it might have been a kitchen at one time, for there was a chimney-breast which could have contained a cooking stove. The room had, however, been turned into an office, complete with filing cabinets and a kneehole desk. In a swivel chair with his feet up on the latter was an officer in the black uniform of the SS. He was fast asleep, and the noise the Saint had heard was him snoring.

The Saint gently closed the door behind him and began to edge his way past the desk towards another door on the far side of the room. He stepped noiselessly but it made no difference. The German officer's head slipped off the cushioning palm of his hand. He gave one last snort and woke up.

The first thing he saw when he opened his eyes was the Saint.

2

Simon Templar was not taken aback or even bothered. He had figured that it would be a long shot if he got by the sleeping soldier. Experience had taught him that most risks could be turned into good chances. If they didn't work out, then one had to improvise something new out of them.

He slipped his pistol from its shoulder holster. Its muzzle covered the startled officer implacably.

"*Guten Tag,*" said the Saint affably. He continued in his fluent German. "I have come to fix your main drain. They tell me you are blocked up. Would you mind removing your clothes?"

In spite of his facetious manner, the Saint's cold blue eyes brooked no argument. Their message was clear.

German officers in long underwear look no more impressive than any other men and just as absurd. Indeed, the purpose of uniforms is primarily to lend dignity where it is not naturally bestowed. This SS officer, who had looked awesome in his black uniform, without it was just a rather heavy-set pot-bellied man.

"*Menschenskind, wie sehen sie aus!*" Simon said unkindly, looking him up and down. "But I suppose all the SS aren't recruited from lingerie models."

Rapidly the Saint got into the other's uniform, contriving to do it without ever letting his Walther waver from its hollow-eyed concentration on its target. The change of costume which had been so unexpectedly offered to him, he figured, could only be a godsend. It was a little short for him; but keeping his labourer's clothes on underneath, and flattening his canvas shoes above the belt under his shirt, helped to make up the equatorial bulk which he lacked. It would have been a disaster if the jackboots had been impossibly small: even he would have found it hard to impersonate an SS officer parading around Schloss Este in his socks. Fortunately, they were not impossibly loose on him, and hid the shortness of the breeches; and the officer's cap was just the right size. Simon put it on at a rakish angle.

The problem now was what to do with his captive.

The Saint was suddenly inspired with an idea straight out of the blue, which could only have been sent by some particularly impish devil to a kindred spirit.

Keeping his prisoner covered, he backed to the window and looked out. His surmise had been right. The room was on the south flank of the Castle, opposite the main entrance. Below it was the cliff which protected the defences on this side and which overhung the village of Este. It was a steep and rugged cliff. An enemy under fire would find it almost impossible to scale. On the other hand, going from top to bottom would be a relatively easy matter, although it might take some time.

Simon beckoned the officer.

"You are about to take a walk, my friend," he said.

The other stared at him with bulging eyes.

"You must be mad."

The Saint walked over to him. He stuck his gun into the man's ribs and prodded him to the window.

"There you are." He pointed downwards. "Take it slowly and you'll have no trouble. Get up too much momentum and you'll have to take your meals off the mantelshelf for a while."

A gleam of hope shone for an instant in the man's eyes. The Saint could tell what was going through his mind. He evidently regarded Simon as a fool for not shooting him out of hand. Once he had got beyond the range of Simon's gun he could raise the alarm. Happily for his peace of mind, he didn't know what the Saint had in store for him.

He gave Simon a scornful look as he climbed through the window and dropped down on to a ledge below. The Saint watched him begin his descent. Much of the cliff consisted of long shale slides. These were not too perilous, although some of them ended in a potentially lethal sheer drop. Nevertheless, there was no reason why the German should not get down safely if he kept his head. All Simon was going to do was to complicate his life for a little while and give him something with which to occupy his mind. After all, one didn't want even members of the SS to get too bored. That would have been unkind. The Saint was all for being kind. He leaned out of the window and fired several shots in the direction of the German, who quickly ducked down behind a big rock.

The shots had the effect he desired. Guards rushed to windows and parapets. Whenever the German showed himself they promptly fired at him, reasonably enough, for no one had any business climbing that cliff up or down, especially a man in his underwear. Anyway, soldiers are not given to asking the whys and wherefores in a top-security situation. They prefer to shoot first, partly because it gives them a chance to do what they are trained to do, and ask or answer questions later. The officer was going to have his work cut out to inch his way down the cliff under fire from his own men. Moreover, the attention of the garrison would be centred on trying to shoot one of their own leaders. The piquancy of the situation struck Simon as purely hilarious, but he couldn't afford to stay and enjoy it. He had to take the maximum advantage of its help as a distraction.

He moved quickly to the door on the far side of the room. Opening it cautiously, he peered through. Had there been anyone on the other side the man would not have known what hit him, for the Saint was ready for fast and decisive action. The room was empty, however. It was apparently an outer office, for it contained a desk, a typewriter, a telephone, and some more filing cabinets. German bureaucracy evidently required a lot of paper work, even in the Gestapo. There should have been an orderly or a secretary about, but he or she was probably having the German equivalent of elevenses: perhaps a stein of lager and a triple-decker leberwurst sandwich.

He walked almost casually across the room. The door on the other side gave on to a landing and a wide flight of stairs leading to the floors above and below. Here there was a storm trooper, but his attention had been seduced by the noise outside, and he was leaning out of a window, the broad expanse of his bottom looking comical in the frame.

Cat-like, the Saint tip-toed across the landing. He took the flight of stairs leading downwards. Although Simon had entered the Castle on the ground floor on the north side, on the cliff side there were several lower floors, and the steps led to a hall on another north side ground floor at a lower level.

Simon went noiselessly down the stairs. They doubled back under themselves, out of sight of the trooper, and after another zig or zag, debouched into a large marble-paved hall, hung with the usual antlered trophies and some old family paintings. One of the portraits, a girl in a ruff and a dress embroidered with pearls, was the image of Frankie. It had that same air of careless arrogance mixed with friendly amusement, a look which said, "You may like me, and I like you, in spite of the fact that I am much better than you are."

Simon halted for a moment to think things out. He was faced with the choice of more doors, all of them closed. Which should he choose to go through? The muted sound of firing still came from above and he could hear the echo of hurrying footsteps in distant corridors. He had no time to waste.

It seemed probable that Frankie would be held in the most inaccessible part of the Castle. That would be in the tower, or even in a dungeon beneath it. Medieval towers were built as keeps—to keep people out, in fact!—in which to make a stand should the rest of the castle be captured. Its inaccessibility could still be used to keep prisoners or secrets in. Simon figured his best bet, therefore, was to head for the keep.

He judged this to be in a direction opposite to the staircase. He traversed the marble floor and opened one of the heavy double doors. He had guessed right. On the other side, the massive walls of a large room still furnished in somewhat medieval style with trestle tables and benches indicated that he had entered the oldest part of the Castle. At the other end of this room, which could well have been the original banqueting hall, stone stairs led upwards and downwards, spiralling as they went.

He was now faced with another decision: whether to look for Frankie in an upstairs chamber, or in a subterranean prison below. He decided that the Teutonic mind would hold that prisoners should be kept in dungeons, and he headed down the stairs.

At the bottom was another passage. The only light came from some tiny windows set high up in the outside wall. These were barred, although they were too small for any adult to get through. A heavy oaken door at the end of the passage was half open. The Saint crept up to it and squinted through.

He was looking into a small anteroom. Two soldiers were seated at a table playing cards. The Saint had caught them in flagrant dereliction of their duty: they were certainly supposed to be on guard, for their guns leant against the table and they must have felt quite sure of being able to hear anybody approaching in time to put away their cards and resume their duty positions.

Simon felt a surge of exhilaration in his always sanguine spirits. Guards, except at royal palaces, where they are largely for show, usually guard something. In this case it was likely that these two were watching over a prisoner: Frankie . . .

From this room another flight of stone steps led downwards, to a dungeon, or perhaps a number of them, the Saint surmised. In the old days, escape from such a set-up, past guards and locked doors, would have been virtually impossible. It was not going to be a cakewalk even now, but for the moment Simon had the initiative.

Pulling down his tunic and adopting a ramrod Prussian air, he stomped into the room, for the first time letting his borrowed boots make the sort of sound they were designed for. The two soldiers looked up with complete consternation writ largely on their countenances. They were so taken aback that they could not even rise to their feet.

The Saint did not give them a chance to pull themselves together. Freezingly he glared at them and then pointed to the dungeon staircase. "Take me to the prisoner," he commanded in his harshest and most arrogant German.

The two men did not question his authority. There was no reason why they should. An SS officer in uniform could only appear in the midst of a Gestapo fortress with the proper accreditation and in fact could only be a real officer in the SS. That was their simple and logical reasoning. They leapt to their feet and hastened downstairs ahead of Simon, babbling abject excuses for their conduct.

At the foot of the steps there was another heavy door. This one had a grille in it. Haughtily the Saint pointed to the lock.

One of the guards produced a large iron key and opened it. Simon waved the soldiers back and strode in.

Frankie was sitting in a corner on a truckle bed. She looked pale and dispirited. She glanced up as the Saint entered, and instantly her posture changed. She gave no sign of recognition, but her back straightened and her chin assumed a disdainful aristocratic angle.

"Come with me. I wish to talk to you," Simon said imperiously, in the bullying tone that he had adopted to fit his uniform.

Grabbing her by the arm, he pulled her to her feet and sent her spinning through the door with such force that she fell heavily outside.

The guards laughed sycophantically at this display of Aryan superiority. Simon allowed them a tight-lipped smile. Then, very deliberately, he kicked one of them on the shins and the other up the backside.

"Imbeciles!" he shouted. "Pigs like you are a disgrace to the Fatherland. You will stand here at attention until I get back, and you had better hope that I shall be in a good mood and will not have you flogged."

Then, holding Frankie by the elbow, he propelled her up the stairs ahead of him.

"Thank you for keeping your head and not giving me away," he whispered as they reached the anteroom.

"I was waiting for you," she said. "I knew you'd come, somehow."

"God save your trusting fat head," said the Saint fervently, as they crossed the room and fled up the flight of stairs to the banqueting hall.

The main hall was still empty, but the sound of firing had ceased. The SS officer must either have got away or be lying low—unless, of course, he had been shot by his own men.

The Saint halted.

"There is a small matter of a necklace," he remarked coolly. "I suppose we might as well pick it up while we're here. I mean, it'll save us another trip. Not that I haven't enjoyed this one. I just love climbing along other people's sewers. But as the saying goes, when you've seen one drain you've seen 'em all."

Surprisingly, Frankie shook her head.

"We have no time and we cannot get to the place where it is. We must try again."

The Saint gave her a long incredulous stare. It was not like Frankie to give up so easily.

"All right," he said finally. "Let's get out of here then. I have my own special entrance and exit."

He led her up the main staircase.

He had intended dealing with the trooper outside the secretary's office in the same way as he had handled the soldiers guarding the dungeon, but the man was no longer there. Simon turned to lead Frankie into the office, and then the door opened.

They found themselves staring into the muzzle of a Mauser machine pistol held by a grim-faced SS corporal.

3

The man lowered his weapon at the sight of the Saint's uniform, and his eyes widened when he saw Frankie.

"*Was geschieht, bitte?*" he asked.

"I am from Central Kontrolle," Simon replied easily. "I have been sent to take the Frau Gräfin back with me. She is an important prisoner. Air Marshal Göring himself wishes to see her in Berlin." He leered professionally. "She is a pretty woman, yes? And the Marshal likes the girls. Perhaps that is the reason."

The soldier remained suspicious.

"Your papers, please sir," he demanded respectfully but firmly.

There were some papers in the inner pocket of the tunic

the Saint was wearing, but Simon felt sure there was no point in trying to pass himself off with them: they would undoubtedly include a photograph which would not resemble him in the least. He must stick to his role of an emissary from Berlin.

"My papers are in my car," he said brusquely. "If you will come along with me to the courtyard I will show them to you."

"To the courtyard?" repeated the corporal.

"Certainly, to the courtyard. I *was* on my way to see your chief. He will be interested to know why my visit has been delayed."

For a moment the soldier looked uncertain.

"You say you come from the Air Marshal in Berlin, sir?" he asked. "But he is . . ."

A curious look came into his eyes and he did not finish his sentence.

"Exactly," said the Saint crisply, "and therefore my mission is urgent. I wish to see your superior officer."

The man smiled, and the Saint did not like that smile. It was the expression of someone who knows something to his own advantage and to someone else's detriment. The someone else in this case could only be the Saint. At any rate, that was the way Simon figured it, and he had a habit of being right.

"Very well, sir," said the soldier, "then we will go together."

He motioned with his gun for the Saint and Frankie to precede him down the stairs.

Simon did not budge.

"I understand this is his office," he said coldly.

"It is, sir, but he is not there. I have just been to look for him myself. We will go to the Kommandant's office. He is the man you should be seeing anyway."

His eyes were cunning and malicious. The Saint liked him less and less and felt sorry for his wife. But then perhaps her eyes were cunning and malicious too. The corporal had the self-satisfied air of one who could already feel the stripes of a *Feldwebel* on his sleeve.

Suddenly, Frankie took off on her own. The Saint cursed inwardly. A moment later he did so outwardly. Frankie dashed for the stairs and the soldier fired a shot in the air.

Simon had to admire the way the man kept his head. It would obviously be awkward for him if he had to report that he had killed this prize prisoner, but it would be even more awkward if he had to announce that she had escaped. If the warning shot failed to halt her, he would have to try to do so by shooting her in the leg.

Frankie kept on going. The soldier aimed his gun at her.

There was nothing for it. The Saint saw what he must do. People were always amazed at how quickly such a big man could move when he wanted to. Greased lightning wasn't in it. Greased time was more like it. One moment he was standing some feet from the soldier and the next, without any apparent movement, he was astride his prone body. The soldier would never be able to recall exactly what had happened, but for some time his slumber would be untroubled by that problem.

Simon grinned rather mirthlessly at Frankie, who had halted in her tracks.

"Magnificent," he said. "Also magnificently stupid. And for Christ's sake, will you stop sticking your neck out and hoping that I'll manage to catch the axe."

He was interrupted from elaborating the lecture by shouts from above and the clattering of feet on the stairs.

They had no choice but to flee downwards. They dashed down the stairs into the front hall. This did not solve their dilemma. They could go through one of the doors which led to other parts of the castle and try to hide somewhere, but it was certain that there would be a thorough search of the whole premises and that would inevitably lead to their capture. It looked as if there was nothing for it but to carry on

into the courtyard and hope somehow to be able to bluff the
sentry at the gate.

The Saint opened the great front door and they slipped
through. He closed the door instantly behind them, in the
hope that the pursuit would be left briefly without a clue as
to which way they had gone.

"Take it easy, old girl," he said to Frankie. "Pretend we
belong here."

"But I do," Frankie said with a smile.

Simon took her arm and marched her boldly out from the
sheltering archway into the open courtyard.

His first impression was that there was a Staff car parked in
the shadows on one side of the square, with a chauffeur in
Luftwaffe uniform industriously polishing the windshield.
This was corrected when he realised it could not possibly be a
Staff car, since it was a Delage D8 100 Mouette saloon with
the famous special body by Henri Chapron—not the sort of
car which an ordinary officer of the German army, or even the
SS, would have at his disposal. It must belong to someone
special.

The Saint scanned the courtyard as he walked towards it.
Aside from the parading guard by the gate the place was
empty. Then suddenly a door in the side wing on his left
opened and two men came out.

One was a slim elegant figure in an SS uniform with a colonel's insignia. Simon guessed he was the Kommandant of the
Castle. He indicated by his posture and general manner extreme deference towards his companion, a large jolly-looking
man in a peaked cap and a greatcoat with two rows of medals
hung on it in violation of the usual regulations for the wearing of decorations.

There was no mistaking the Prime Minister of Prussia,
Chief of the Luftwaffe, and, so rumour had it, Director of the
Four Year Plan for War Preparations. And he knew now why
that officious corporal had become so smug.

For Simon Templar it was suddenly spring. It was a lovely

day and everything was happening just right. There was nothing that would lend more zest to that moment than an encounter with one of the most formidable chiefs of the Nazi Reich. It struck him that the Air Marshal's presence in the Castle could even be connected with the Hapsburg Necklace. Simon's earlier improvisations might have hit the nail on the head. The Nazi leader might want to find the Necklace for the benefit of the Third Reich, but he was also known to be a greedy and insatiable collector of art and antiques. The Necklace might well end up round his wife's neck—or perhaps even his own, in view of his well-known liking for decorations. Unless they knew what it was, nobody would ask any questions. Even if anyone did, this man's power and influence were sufficient to ensure that such questions were not asked out loud.

Holding Frankie by the arm, Simon hurried her across the courtyard to meet the approaching officials by the Delage. The chauffeur looked startled. The SS colonel was obviously completely flummoxed. His jaw fell open and the monocle dropped out of his eye. The Minister alone remained apparently unmoved by this sudden and extraordinary encounter.

"*Ach, mein lieber Freund!*" cried the Saint, with genial familiarity. "How nice to see you again! And how is dear Emma and all the children? Are they all at Schloss Harinhall?"

"Who are you?" asked the Minister guardedly.

His smile was broad and tolerant, but his eyes, with their pin-prick pupils, were as cold as dry ice.

"Oh, don't pay any attention to this uniform," replied the Saint jovially, as he opened the door for Frankie to get in. "I won it off a chap at strip poker. Surely you remember me? I'm Cardinal Spaghetti, Chief of the Vatican Plumbing Department. This is my wife."

As he spoke he swung himself into the driving seat of the Delage, having already seen that the key was in the ignition. A car of this kind and in such a guarded place would be considered safe. After all, it was inconceivable that anyone would try to steal such an important vehicle in such a stronghold. Anyone but the Saint . . .

The Kommandant swore and lunged for the door. The chauffeur stood there with a look of complete astonishment on his face. From his point of view the fact that a member of the SS and a woman had taken over his master's car was obviously quite beyond his comprehension. As the car shot away, Simon looked in the driving mirror and saw that Göring was actually convulsed with laughter, and he realised why this man was such a formidable figure in the political hierarchy of his country. The aristocratic detachment which allowed a sense of humour to operate in a situation of this sort was something not even Hitler possessed, let alone the rest of the vulgar and common men who headed the Nazis and the Third Reich.

The car roared through the outer gateway. The startled sentry saluted it and Simon's uniform smartly. The SS officer shouted at him to stop the car, but by that time it was rounding the corner of the Castle wall and a moment later it was out of sight.

The Saint slowed down a little for the next bend.

"No point in killing ourselves," he murmured. "Besides, we have to pick up Leopold."

"Where is he?"

"Sitting on a sharp stone farther down the hill meditating. He's finally decided to get down to fundamentals."

Simon stopped the car beside the rock slide and got out and stood beside it. He waved and called, "Come out and play, Leopold. It's me, Simon. Hurry up, or you'll miss the bus and there isn't another one."

A moment later Leopold emerged from behind a rock and scrambled up the avalanche towards them. He was carrying the two satchels.

"What does this mean?" he panted. "And that uniform—"

"Explanations later," said the Saint curtly. "We've got half the German army on our tail. Pile in and let's get going."

Leopold climbed into the back seat and stowed the bags on the floor at his feet. The Saint got back in the car and launched it off again.

"*Gott Sei Dank*, Frankie!" chattered Leopold from the back seat. "How did you escape?"

"Simon got me out, of course," Frankie told him impatiently. "But we are still escaping. They are bound to come after us."

"And the Necklace?"

"Is still safe."

Leopold's snort of exasperation with Frankie's dictatorial and dismissive manner could be heard over the noise of engine, tyres, and the wind of their passage.

"How far are they behind you, Simon?" he wanted to know.

"Still a fair way, I should think," answered the Saint calmly. "It'd have to take them a few minutes to turn out a posse and get it carborne, and I shouldn't think their transportation department's got anything that has the legs of this job. Our problem is that I still can't drive as fast as words can go through a telephone wire."

"I know a back road that will avoid the next town," Frankie said. "Probably they don't know it—it's not much more than a cart track—"

"But first, darling," Simon reminded her, "we've got to get past the guards at the entrance to this *verboten* area."

They zoomed through the hamlet of Este, scattering geese and peasant children from their path. As they left the village behind, Leopold said: "We should have gone back through the drain, as we came in."

"We couldn't," said the Saint. "The hut we hid in is in full view of the Castle, and by this time the battlements are crawling with characters on the lookout. Some sniper would have earned himself an Iron Cross before we got near it. Anyway, Frankie wouldn't like the drain. There's no class to it."

Frankie smiled at him.

"I think you just like this car."

"It's a beauty," he admitted. "And was lent to me by a very distinguished owner."

"But how do we get out of the camp? They'll be waiting for us at the gate and we can't just climb over the barbed wire."

The Saint shrugged.

"I won't know till I see what the set-up is when we get to the gate."

"We're there now," she said, pointing ahead.

The gate was closed. Four soldiers crouched in front of it. What was more important was that they were crouching over machine-guns. The phone call which he had anticipated had reached them in time enough. If ever there was a situation where he had to improvise, it was there.

His genius did not let him down. As it neared the boundary fence, the road ran beside a grassy field. The Saint drove a little nearer to the gate and then swung the car off into the field so that it was at right angles to the road with its back towards the machine-gun squad, who were scrambling to turn the guns through a ninety-degree realignment. But they had not yet opened fire, perhaps because they had been ordered to take live prisoners if possible.

"Get down on the floor," he ordered Leopold and Frankie.

Then he crouched down low over the wheel and reversed full tilt towards the machine-guns and their attendants.

He knew that there was a good chance that he might be dead in the course of the next few seconds, but the chances of death were paradoxically all that they had to live for. He had to gamble on the unexpectedness of his manoeuvre, the awkwardness of the machine-gun mounts, the probability that Göring's car would have been equipped with some non-standard bullet-proofing, and the fact that the rear-wheel transmission was much less liable to disablement by impact than the front-wheel steering.

The astonished soldiers did not have time to get their guns properly trained and only managed a few wild bursts of sporadic fire before the Delage was upon them. There was a succession of splintering crashes as the car knocked their machine-guns for six. There was a nasty lurch as one of the wheels went over a soldier who failed to get out of its way. Simon spun the wheel full lock, and there came a tremendous crash as the car hurtled backwards through the gates.

On the other side of them the Saint wrenched it through another three-point turn and sent it barrelling away down the highway towards potential freedom. A few scattered shots reached his ears from behind, but he heard only two or three bullets hit the coachwork.

"You can come out now," he told Frankie and Leopold. "The storm is past and there will be *thé dansant* in the lounge."

"*Mein Gott,*" said Leopold, climbing back on to his seat. "Sometimes I think you must be a maniac."

"If I weren't," said the Saint, "I'd never have got into this caper."

4

They were soon out of the hills, and as they drove along a rutted lane in flat countryside the Saint considered what to do next.

"I think," he said, "our best bet is to head for a border post and take it from there. We've got to get back into Austria and contact Max. If we're lucky we'll be able to talk our way through, if not—well, there's always the odd miracle if you've led a good life like I have."

"If you've led a good life," Frankie said, "Machiavelli should be made a saint."

"Only I beat him to it," Simon reminded her.

"I don't like it," Leopold said darkly. "We shall all be arrested and shot."

"Oh, Leopold, you are always so negative," Frankie protested.

"As the model said to the photographer," flipped the Saint. "At any rate this crate lives up to its prospectus. They say it'll do a hundred without turning a hair, although on a track like this it hasn't much of a chance. But this Cotal electric gearbox is very convenient." He accelerated rapidly after a skidding turn. "We ought to get somewhere pretty fast as long as we keep her filled up and remember to cough in the tyres every now and then."

"Exactly!" said Leopold, in a voice which sounded both gloomy and supercilious.

"What does that mean?" demanded Frankie.

"Yes," Simon seconded. "'Exactly' may be precise, but it also leaves one neither here nor there. All over the place, so to speak, and not anywhere in particular."

"Have you looked at the petrol gauge recently?" Leopold asked sourly.

The Saint looked.

"Hmmm. Yes, I see what you mean. Rather low. They must have hit the tank when they were shooting at us, the naughty boys. Let's hope the puncture isn't right at the bottom. Well, have faith, as the Good Book says, and ye shall move internal combustion engines. I'm sure Moses didn't worry about petrol pumps."

"Yes, but he was walking," Frankie said.

"And so may we be shortly," responded the Saint. "Onward Christian soldiers, and all that. It's an idea. We can arrive at the border on bare feet and say we're pilgrims headed for Berlin to lay a wreath on the tomb of the Unknown Rabbi. That ought to get us the red carpet treatment, though I'd rather not wonder what they'd dye it with."

"We shall soon be on a better road," Frankie said, and they were.

They tore through a poverty-stricken village of strangely oriental-looking dirty whitewashed hovels. Some children and old peasants watched their passage with amazement, their interest making their slant Magyar eyes almost round.

Glancing at the fuel gauge every few seconds, Simon saw that the level was falling much faster than even extravagant consumption would account for, although not so fast as to reveal a catastrophic outpour. Therefore they should have quite a few miles still in hand—but the precise number would depend entirely on the level at which the tank had been perforated. If the damage was high up enough, the leak might stop by itself while they had a few gallons left; but if it was right at the bottom, the tank would very soon run dry. They were "ifs" with the palm-sweating uncertainty of Russian roulette.

Simon decided that it was worth wasting a precious minute to know the worst—or the best. He brought the car to a stop, got out, and ran back to kneel in the road behind it.

In little more than a minute he was back in the driver's seat and starting off again.

"The hole in the tank is very low down and pretty big," he reported almost conversationally. "I stuffed a handkerchief in it, but we'd lose as much petrol as we'd save while we were trying to make a better patch. We'll just have to keep our fingers crossed and see how far we go."

"There you are!" said Leopold lugubriously. "I told you this whole idea was crazy."

"You are a man of very sound if limited judgment," Simon assured him consolingly.

"No, we have a good chance," Frankie contradicted. "I know this road, and the border post is now only a few kilometres away."

"Yes," said Leopold darkly, "and what happens then?

They stop us and ask for our papers, and while they are examining them the Gestapo catches up with us."

He passed his finger across his throat expressively, as Simon saw in the rear-view mirror. To Simon Templar, the gesture was an irresistible provocation.

"Quite right," he assented heartily. "Sound, if limited, again. Besides, they're bound to have reported this car missing. Every official from here to Berchtesgarten will be watching out for it. Now if you've got any other jolly thoughts to boost our morale, do let us share them."

Leopold lapsed into aggrieved silence, and the Saint drove steadily on at the best speed he could estimate as a compromise between the need to evade pursuit and the need to conserve fuel.

Presently the winding but improved lane that they were on ended abruptly in a T-junction with what was obviously a main road.

"We've done it!" claimed Frankie excitedly. "Turn right, and the frontier is only about two kilometres."

It was just as Simon braked for the turn that the engine coughed, started up again, coughed, ran for a few seconds, and then died.

"Well," said the Saint, "that's that. Don't say anything, Leopold. This is no time for sound if limited pronouncements. What we need is another miracle. I have it! *Cogito ergo sum*—the old cogs are going round." He leapt out of the car. "Come on, Leopold. Bring my bag of tools, and make sure it's mine."

A moment later he had exposed the engine of the Delage and was working on the carburettor with a spanner from the tool kit. When he had the top off he reached into the bag again and pulled out the brandy bottle. He unscrewed the top and took a swig.

"*Prost*," he said, and poured the rest of the cognac into the carburettor.

"*Gott im Himmel!*" squealed Frankie, who was leaning out of the car window to watch.

"Now I know you are mad!" exploded Leopold.

"I admit it's a bit of a waste," said the Saint calmly. "Delamain '14 wasn't exactly meant for use in cars. But it always pays to have the best."

"But surely a car won't run on brandy?" said Frankie.

"A car will run on anything that's got enough alcohol in it. I'm sure that Delamain won't let us down. After all, it's a mature and brave spirit, as they say."

"And how far will that get us?"

"Hardly anywhere," said the Saint cheerfully, as he squeezed behind the wheel again. "But that's where we're going. Come on, Leopold, don't bother about the tools. Pile in!"

Simon pressed the starter, and the motor sprang to life almost immediately. He put the car in gear and started off.

As he began to turn out of the lane, he had to brake quickly to give way to a black Audi saloon that came speeding along the main road from their left. There were three men in it, in civilian clothes, and the two who were not driving turned automatically to glance at the Delage as they swept past.

Simon glimpsed on their faces a much more startled reaction than the situation warranted. And there was something about the character of the faces themselves, combined with the character of the car, that spelled out just one word in his brain.

The word went into italics when the Audi's stop lights blazed red and the car swerved sharply to the righthand verge and then swung into an abrupt left turn across the highway and stopped, effectively blocking the road.

"*Gestapo!*" the Saint said aloud.

Without an instant's hesitation, he let the clutch in again and spurred the Delage forward with all the acceleration of which it was capable.

"Hold tight, Leo," he barked, and flung out his own right arm like a bar across Frankie's chest to prevent her being hurled through the windscreen when the crash came.

It came, and he was ready for it with his feet braced against the firewall, and his tremendous strength held Frankie back enough to save her from contact with dashboard or windscreen. The Delage had not attained a speed at which no preparedness could have spared them the effects of a collision, but the crunch was still sickeningly loud. The side of a car is infinitely more vulnerable than the front, and the Audi was hit broadside just as the men in it were opening the doors to get out. The Audi was slammed two feet squarely sideways and almost rocked over.

The Saint was out of the Delage the instant he had assured himself that Frankie was unhurt. Of the two shocked Gestapo men left in the Audi, he chose the one who looked liveliest to yank out first, and destroyed that unseemly sprightliness with a left to the solar plexus and a sledgehammer chop to the back of the neck. The second, with a nasty cut over one eye, was moaning dazedly, and Simon compassionately put him out of his pain with a carefully placed uppercut. The third, who had been farthest out of the Audi when the Delage hit it, had probably been caught and crushed by the collapsing door: he lay face up in the road, looking as if he would give no trouble for a long time, if ever.

Within seconds, the menace of the *Geheimnisstadtspolizei* had been at least temporarily neutralised. But so also had the services of the Reichmarshal's elegant Delage.

Simon rejoined Frankie and Leopold, who were now standing beside it.

"Have we got anything to tie up some partypoopers?" he asked.

Leopold looked blank. Frankie furrowed her brow in thought.

"I am wearing three petticoats," she said. "I think I could

spare a couple, and there are always my stockings. They're thick wool and serviceable."

"The best possible service for them," Simon approved. "Peasant girls are very well equipped in every sense of the word, apparently. Come on, Leopold, let's arrange our patients while Frankie takes off her clothes."

In a minute or two Frankie joined them. She handed Simon her stockings and a fancy petticoat of the kind peasant girls saved for special occasions when they might display them in high-kicking and swinging folk dances. With the help of his knife the Saint swiftly ripped it into strips. The men were soon tied and gagged and arranged in a neat triangle, head to foot. Simon placed the empty brandy bottle in the centre, like a hub.

"I do like to leave things tidy," he remarked, and even Leopold smiled.

The two interlocked wrecks blocked the road like two grappling dinosaurs that had expired in mortal combat. Simon patted the Delag apologetically on its crumpled bonnet.

"Even if you died on a drunken binge, remember it was a '14 cognac," he said.

He was stripping off his SS uniform with the rapidity of a quick-change artiste. It went into the ditch, along with the jackboots, and he put the more comfortable canvas shoes back on his feet.

He set off at such a fast pace that the other two had difficulty in keeping up. Once they were over the brow of a low hill they could see the border station quite clearly. It was the usual type, consisting of a shed and a barrier bar across the road, weighted at one end so that it could be raised or lowered easily. The bar was in its blocking position.

Simon kept going without breaking stride.

"Don't let it look as if we were a bit concerned," he said. "The sportsmen we just took out of play must have been the Gestapo detail sent to watch for us at the border. With any luck, the regular border guards will only have been told to look out for a peasant girl and a man in SS uniform. How did you get across, Frankie?"

"My papers say I'm a Hungarian waitress working at a *gasthaus* near the border in Austria. I was just coming on a visit to my family."

"Okay. So now you're going back to work. And no reason why a couple of agricultural-engineer customers that you ran into shouldn't walk you back."

The Saint paused and considered the immediate future thoughtfully. "Well," he said finally, "I think this is going to be a case of brains over brawn. Come on, let's see if we can talk our way through."

"I think you'd better let me do the talking," said Frankie. "After all, I speak Hungarian as my second language."

"And I speak it as my eighth," laughed the Saint, "but I'm not going to talk Hungarian. You just wait and see!"

Frankie looked doubtful and worried. Leopold looked doubtful and annoyed. So far the Saint had come through with flying colours, but the young man was always looking for a possible slip-up on the part of the man he both admired and resented. But if the Saint had any misgivings they could only have been perceived by a lie detector.

Arm in arm with Frankie, he marched unhesitatingly up to the border post. It was manned by two men in uniform who regarded them with little interest. One of them held out his hand with a supercilious expression for the Saint's papers. He did not even bother to ask for them. But the other gave Frankie a slight smile of recognition.

"Was your family well," he inquired in Hungarian.

"Very well, thank you," she replied in the same language.

"It was not a long visit."

"It was only to settle some family business. And my mother was glad I could go back with these friends."

The barrier was raised, and they were waved on. It was as easy as that.

The Austrian barrier was about twenty yards ahead.

"Keep your fingers crossed, and your eyes too," said the Saint. "We're halfway home."

The Austrian station was manned by two guards who watched their approach across no-man's-land through a window in their small official building. As Frankie and her companions reached it, one guard stepped out to meet them, holding a rifle in the crook of his arm.

"*Ihre Urkunde, bitte.*"

Each of them produced the documents that Annellatt had provided.

The guard took them with one hand, glanced at them, and then transferred them to two fingers of the hand which cradled his rifle, so that he could take a notebook from his pocket and consult it.

A very small semblance of an ominous smile came to his thin lips.

"These papers are forgeries," he stated flatly. "We have been waiting for someone to present them."

V

How maternity became Frankie, and there were puns and punishment

1

If ever there was a moment when the Saint experienced in all its classic cosmicality the emotion of a man who has literally had a rug pulled from under him, this was it. Perhaps his heart did not actually stop beating, but it would have had to be a mindless mechanical device not to have faltered. Somehow he maintained a superhuman control of his expression, but for a moment he could do nothing about the leaden numbness which seemed to spread from somewhere around his midriff to threaten his mental resilience.

Of all the possible hazards and difficulties that he had vaguely anticipated and had been in a general way prepared to cope with, this was the last and least considered in his elastic contingency plans.

"That is impossible," he protested automatically. "There must be some mistake."

Even as he said it, he knew how hollow his bluster must sound, and how unavailing it must be.

"There is no mistake," said the guard coldly, and made the slightest motion of his head at the control building.

His certainty was granite-like. No histrionic bluff could have ever scratched it. He had been tipped off beyond range of peradventure.

Someone in Herr Annellatt's "organisation" had spilled the beans, and the spillage had been efficiently broadcast. But it would do no good, then and there, to speculate on the identity of the spiller.

The other guard was coming out of the control building in response to the first guard's nod. He had an automatic pistol holster on his belt, and his right hand rested on the open flap.

The Saint recovered as a professional boxer does after taking a near-knockout punch. Though it had seemed like an eternity to him, the duration of his paralysis would have had to be measured in fractioned seconds. And while his brain told him that there was no intellectual way out of this situation, his physical reflexes, like those of any professional, made him come back fighting.

The guard with the rifle was still tucking his notebook back in his pocket, and the hand he had near the trigger was still encumbered by the papers he was holding. Simon grabbed the barrel of the rifle and yanked it towards him while he drove one knee into the guard's groin. The rifle came loose, and the Saint added his right hand to another grip on it with which he whirled it like an airplane propeller to slam the butt stunningly against the side of the man's head.

The other guard's hand had barely touched the butt of his holstered pistol when the Saint had him almost impaled at the stomach on the muzzle of the captured rifle. The man froze in instant terror, but the Saint was not quite ruthless enough to touch the trigger. On the other hand, he could see no asset value in such a prisoner. So he reconciled humanitarian scruples and practical considerations by merely driving the muzzle in harder and then bringing the rifle butt over in another propeller spin that ended on the guard's left temple with a clout that could not fail to discount his participation for at least an hour.

"I just don't understand it," Simon mourned, looking down at the two uninterested guards. "Everywhere I go, I seem to run into violence. What is the world coming to?"

Frankie and Leopold were staring at him as if they were still trying to wake up.

Simon threw down the rifle and took Frankie's arm again.

"Come on," he said. "These little interruptions are a nuisance, but we shouldn't let them spoil our trip."

There was no vehicle of any kind parked around the border post, from which he concluded that the guards were relieved at intervals by some circulating vehicle which deposited a fresh detail and carted the previous couple off to their well- or un-earned rest.

With a cheery wave of his hand to the gaping Hungarians on the other side of the neutral zone, he hustled Frankie and Leopold past the barrier and down the road at an easy jog-trot. Within a hundred yards a curve took both frontier posts out of sight.

"How long before we have a chance of being picked up by some friendly soul who hasn't come through the border crossings and been warned about us?" he asked Frankie.

"Very soon we join a main road which is all Austrian," she answered. "This road is just a branch from it to the frontier."

In fact it was less than a quarter of a mile till they connected with the highway. Frankie pointed in the direction which a signpost indicated as leading to Gänserndt, Bad Altenberg, the Neusiedler See, Rust, and points south, and Simon slackened the pace he was setting to a brisk walk.

"It'd look a bit suspicious if we were seen running," he said. "And anyhow we're going to need something to take us a bit faster than feet."

"I think," Frankie said, "I am going to have a baby."

"Bully for you," said the Saint abstractedly, his mind still casting around the enigma of who had blown their fictitious identities. "Will you name it after me?"

He was suddenly grabbed by the shoulder from behind, with a fierceness that brought him up short and turned him around.

"You swine!" Leopold shouted, and came at him with flailing arms.

"Take it easy," Simon murmured, catching him by the front of his shirt and holding him off with ease. "What's all the excitement about? Simon's a good name, unless you're bothered by its non-Aryan origin."

Frankie was almost collapsing with laughter.

"It's all right, Leopold," she gasped. "Simon is not the father. Nobody is."

"Sounds positively biblical," remarked the Saint, turning Leopold loose.

"It will not do us much good to try 'hitch-hiking,' as I have seen it in American films," Frankie explained. She raised the hem of her dress and stuck her leg out in a provocative pose. "They would misunderstand that in Austria. No, we must stop the first driver who comes along and tell him that I must get to the hospital quickly because I am going to have a baby."

The Saint looked at her critically.

"I'm not an expert in these matters, but do you really look the part? I mean, expectant motherhood does make ladies . . . er . . . bloom a bit usually, doesn't it?"

"Don't be silly," snorted Frankie. "Stop a driver and tell him I'm a hospital case, and he's not going to start taking my measurements. Anyway, in this peasant costume, you couldn't really tell, could you?"

The Saint had to admit that she was right. What was more, her idea was a good one. He looked back over his shoulder.

"Well, this is a chance to try it," he said.

A large truck was thundering up behind them, headed in the direction of Rust. Getting into the act, Leopold stepped into the road and flagged it down. The driver stuck his head out of the cab window.

"*Was geschieht?*" he asked.

Leopold pointed to Frankie who was being supported by Simon's arm and looked as if she was enjoying it.

"My wife," he said loudly. "She is having a child. We must get her to the hospital in Rust."

The driver laughed.

"It is a very suitable place."

Simon was amused by the joke, for he was aware that Rust was a town noted as a dwelling place for storks and boasted a stork's nest for every chimney.

The driver jerked his thumb at the Saint.

"Who is he?"

"He is my cousin from Munich." Leopold was learning fast. Simon was not so much a good teacher as a marvellous example. "But he is not a doctor or a midwife."

At that moment Frankie let out a loud moan and swayed on her feet.

"I don't have room for three." The driver leaned over and opened the door of the cab. "If you want him to go too, one of you will have to get in the back."

"We all will," Simon said agreeably. "Then we can look after the woman if things start to happen."

The driver shrugged and slammed the door shut. The trio hurried around to the back and climbed into the open truck.

"Right," Simon signalled to the driver. "Full speed ahead."

They drove on down the road at a fast clip. As they went, Simon was watching for the eventually inevitable pursuit, but there was still no sign of it.

It did not take them long to reach Rust.

"Where is the hospital?" inquired the driver, leaning out of the cab window and looking backwards at his passengers.

"I have no idea," shouted Simon over the noise of the engine and the rattle of the chassis, "but if you let us off we'll find it."

"No, no," replied the man. "I will help you get the woman there. We can always ask a policeman."

"I shall ask St Peter if you don't look where you're going," Simon told him, and the man turned round just in time to avoid running into a telephone pole.

Farther along, the driver stopped and asked a peasant carrying two milk pails filled with dung on a wooden yoke over his shoulders the route to the hospital. The man, who looked older than he probably was, as is so ofen the case with peasants, said he knew of no hospital.

"Where is the police station then?" inquired the driver.

For an Austrian peasant the man was admirably and efficiently concise.

"Down the road, first left, second right and third left."

He spat and plodded off, his back indicating that he had had enough idle chatter for one day. The Saint wondered whether his pails would get scrubbed out and sterilised before being used for milk later on. He guessed probably not.

The driver ground the truck's gears and moved off. He seemed incapable of proceeding at less than a breakneck speed.

"Get ready to jump out," Simon told the others. "We'll go when he slows up round the next corner."

He did not even have to lower his voice. The groaning of the engine and banging of the truck's body effectively prevented the driver from hearing anything to arouse his suspicions as they all three slid to the back of the truck and got ready to jump.

As Simon figured it, in making a left-hand turn across the road the man would use the small mirror on his front mudguard on the left side, which would show him only the outside of the truck. Of course, it was possible, even likely, that he would also glance in the rear-view mirror above his windscreen, but that was a chance they would have to take. With any luck he would be a typical Austrian driver and conduct himself as if no one else were on the road.

Fortune was with them, and the driver was in a hurry. His outside mirror showed him plainly that there was no one overtaking him, and he cut across the road towards a side street. As he did so, the Saint and his companions dropped off the back of the truck. Leopold caught Frankie as she stumbled, and the three of them watched the truck vanish behind the corner. No one paid any attention to them, as if this was not an abnormal way for hitch-hikers to abandon their conveyance.

Simon was amused to picture the driver's expressions, both facial and verbal, when he got to the police station and found his passengers gone. But there was also a graver side to the matter. Policemen are always serious and always curious. They are paid to be so. The driver's description of the missing hitch-hikers would cause the police to make enquiries on their network and broadcast their descriptions. And by now the Saint and his companions would be officially very much "wanted." Simon decided that they had better play it safe and get out of Rust as quickly as possible and take the back roads without trying for any more hitch-hiking, while heading for their rendezvous with Max's henchman. The journey was not all that far and, as he put it to the others, a little exercise would do them no harm and might even be of benefit.

Though not far in actual distance, the journey took them much longer than they expected. As far as possible they avoided the roads in case they might be seen and recognised as fugitives. Even rural farmhouses in Austria were likely to have radios. They tramped through muddy fields and forged their way through underbrush. Occasionally they had to hide from people. Once they even sought refuge in a pigsty. This episode lasted for quite a long time, since a farmer brought his horse into a neighbouring field and spent an unconscionable time schooling it. When he finally left the animal to its own devices, they were all three suffering from lack of oxygen and prolonged exposure to an almost insufferable smell.

"Shan't stay at that hotel again," remarked the Saint as they emerged from their hiding place. "Ozone is all very well but it can be overdone. Anyway, if it's smells one wants, the sulphur baths at Baden are just as odoriferous but a lot more comfortable."

Since Leopold knew something of the terrain he acted as their pathfinder, using the compass he had been provided with.

"Just like Max," Frankie said when Simon had finished his tale of how he and Leopold had crossed over to Schloss Este and where they were headed now. "He is a great organiser but he always only goes so far. I think he never finishes a plan because he doesn't want to tie himself down in case anything goes wrong. It's the typical peasant mentality. He always wants to have several ways out."

"So do I," said Simon. "One way in and several ways out. That's always the best set-up—including prison."

"Have you tried, prison I mean?" she asked teasingly.

"Not seriously, but I wouldn't mind one day. It would be a challenge. I mean, one of the really tough ones—Dartmoor or even Alcatraz. Some place where escapes are considered virtually impossible." His eyes had a faraway look. "Maybe the Lubjianka in Moscow, or Devil's Island."

Frankie gazed at him sidelong.

"You are a strange man. Danger is your life's blood, and the impossible your only ambition."

The Saint grinned at her.

"Oh, I have a few others. Like having a quiet *diner à deux* with you some day, some place where none of the Ungodly would be butting in. Where would you fancy?"

"Excuse me," interrupted Leopold with heavy politeness, "but it is getting near sunset and we should hurry a little. It will be difficult to get through the forest after nightfall."

"Och aye, laddie," replied the Saint docilely. "The camels are coming, as the Arab's wife said when he inquired about her dowry. So are we. On, on, and the Devil take the hindquarters."

He laughed at the expression of baffled exasperation on the young man's face.

It had in fact been dark for some time when the rushing waters of the stream they had crossed only twenty-four hours before (although it seemed like days ago) filled the night with their deep-toned chatter.

Simon found the place where the rowing boat had been moored and from there led on upstream until they came to the pylon which Max had told him would be a landmark. They had, in fact, come in a vast full circle.

As Max had also said, from the pylon they could see a log cabin. Its windows were lighted squares in the enshrouding darkness. It struck the Saint as being an interesting coincidence that Max should own a farm so near to Schloss Este. Or had he perhaps purchased it for that very reason?

Simon tried the door, which opened without a creak on well-oiled hinges. The cottage was evidently used frequently or had been especially prepared for their coming.

Simon led the way in.

2

Anton was standing in the middle of the room. His air of nervous apprehension changed to a welcoming smile as he recognised the Saint.

"Good evening, sir," he cried. "Ach, Gräfin Francesca and Graf Leopold! I am thankful to see you all."

"And how glad I am to see you, Anton!" exclaimed Frankie.

A wood fire was burning in the grate and the aromatic scent of scorching resin filled the room, which was comfortably furnished with a sofa, some armchairs, and a table with chairs to go with it. There was no carpet on the floor but the room was scrupulously clean and had a cosy appearance. On the far side were two doors, which the Saint figured probably led to a bedroom and a kitchen respectively. When Simon asked him, Anton confirmed that they did.

Frankie sank into one of the armchairs.

"My God, I'm tired," she said. "I could sleep for a week."

She kicked her shoes off and began rubbing her feet. Leopold went over to the fire and held his hands out to it.

"It is nice to be warm again," he said with feeling.

"My master told me to ask you to rest comfortably here until he sends for you," said Anton. "Perhaps you would all like some food and drink?"

"You are a mind-reader, Anton," beamed the Saint.

The old servant smiled.

"No, sir, just long training."

He went to a sideboard in a corner and fetched out a bottle of Jaegermeister. Soon its mellow fire was coursing through their veins. Anton provided them with a meal of the ubiquitous *leberwurst*, ham, cheese and black bread, but there was also some marvellously fresh butter and a cold game pie with a glazed golden crust to turn the occasion into a feast. They ate in silence, concentrating their whole attention on what they were doing in the manner of starving people. Anton tactfully withdrew into the kitchen and left them to themselves and their repast.

Finally Leopold gave a sigh and pushed back his chair.

"That," he said, stretching out his legs, "was the most beautiful meal I have ever had. It was almost worth the whole adventure."

Frankie looked at him affectionately.

"You are still a child, Leopold. Your stomach means everything to you."

The youth showed a rare gleam of humour.

"Not everything," he said with a grin.

She laughed.

"I love you, Leopold—when you are not being serious."

"I am only serious about you, Frankie," he said directly.

"Well, you shouldn't be." She seemed anxious to change the subject but feminine enough not to let it go too easily.

"Serious, I mean. People who are serious are usually dull. Is that not so, Simon?"

"No," answered the Saint, expanding his sinewy frame in a sudden cat-like movement, his arms behind his head. "I don't find them dull at all. The ones I meet are usually quite seriously out to get me. They may be a nuisance but they are not dull."

Frankie gave him a quizzical look. "I think you are trying to be tactful. But if we must be serious, what do we do now?"

Simon smiled at her. When he was in the right mood, the Saint's smile could be quite an experience for ladies on the receiving end. Frankie blushed, as the personality of this strange man seemed physically to envelop her. Watching them, Leopold fidgeted and did not attempt to conceal his jealousy.

"I'll find out from Anton when he expects to hear from Max," replied the Saint. "But first, tell us how you came to be captured by the Gestapo." His tone and manner brooked no argument. "No more holding out. We've waited for it too long already."

She met his challenging gaze with bland composure.

"I arranged it."

Leopold sat straight up in his chair.

"You did *what?*"

"I wanted them to capture me. In fact, I wasn't really captured at all. I just walked up to the guards at the outer gate and told them who I was. They telephoned the Castle and they were kind enough to send a whole squad of soldiers to escort me. The Germans are always very respectful when it comes to dealing with people of title."

The Saint nodded approvingly.

"That was a very good touch. What better way of getting into the Castle than to get your enemies actually to compel you to go in."

"That's what I thought."

"But what good did you think that was going to do?" protested Leopold. "Surely you couldn't have imagined that they would let you wander about unguarded? You must have known they would put you straight into a dungeon."

Her smile mocked him.

"I did—and they did just that."

He flushed angrily.

"Then you are a complete idiot—*eine dumme Gans!* It is typical of you. You go through life thinking people will always come along and pull you out of whatever mess you get into."

"Which is just what you both did," Frankie said sweetly.

Leopold stuttered with rage.

"You . . . you . . . are totally irresponsible! You don't mind what trouble you cause to others just as long as you get your way. We might have been captured or even killed!"

Frankie wafted a smile in the Saint's direction. "Do you agree?"

Simon nodded.

"He's dead right, but you're pretty enough to get away with it."

She was obviously pleased with the compliment, especially as it came from him. In spite of that, she shook her head.

"But I am not so irresponsible as you both think."

"No?" The Saint's eyebrows were raised satirically.

"No, no!" she reiterated, her eyes wide with excitement that she was finding it harder and harder to suppress.

"Oh no?" sneered Leopold. "All you've done is to put the Germans in Schloss Este on their guard, nearly get us killed, and turn us into fugitives. I tell you, I am not used to this sort of thing and I don't like it unless there is a good reason for it. What you hoped to achieve I can't imagine."

"This!" she said proudly, flinging back the shawl from her neck and shoulders.

The jewels in the Hapsburg Necklace flashed and glinted on her bosom with a brilliance that made them seem alive.

3

Leopold could only gape at her.

The Saint exhaled a breath of utter joy and delight.

"Very neat," he remarked. "And very dramatic too. You'd make a sensational actress and an even better producer. Your sense of timing is perfect."

"But . . . but . . ." stammered Leopold. "Where . . . how . . . how did you get it?"

Her smile was wicked.

"I just went straight to the place where it was."

"You couldn't have. They put you into a dungeon. You told us so yourself!"

"Exactly."

"All right then, how did you get out?"

She was like a cat playing with an irritated mouse, Simon thought. He was amused by the quaintness of his simile. He gave Frankie a conspiratorial wink.

"I got her out," he told the frustrated young man.

"I know that!" exploded Leopold. "I mean how did she get out before you came along?"

"I didn't," Frankie said demurely.

Leopold stamped his foot furiously.

"Stop playing games! This is a serious business, and you have caused enough trouble already without trying to turn it all into a joke."

"I think," murmured Simon, "that you'd better come clean, Frankie, before your cousin has a seizure."

The girl's smile made a bond between them.

"He really should be intelligent enough to guess. You have, haven't you, Simon?"

He nodded.

"But I'm an old rogue, much versed in the ways of the wicked, even when they are beautiful girls."

She turned to Leopold.

"You really are a stupid idiot," she said unkindly but without malice. "Do you mean to tell me that you've no idea?"

"I am no longer playing your game," he said sullenly.

"Leopold, stop behaving like a spoilt child."

"I think," interjected the Saint, "that he wouldn't mind if you were to thank him for all the trouble he went to to get you out of the Castle."

Frankie jumped up and flung her arms around Leopold and kissed him.

"Thank you, thank you, *mein Schatz!* I am very naughty, but I am truly grateful, and you were very brave."

Leopold went a brick red, but he could not help being honest.

"It was not all me," he said, glancing over at Simon.

Frankie triumphantly took up a position in front of the fire.

"All right then, I'll tell you."

"You do just that," the Saint pursued her sardonically.

Frankie was enjoying her moment of glory, which she had been looking forward to.

"It's really so simple if you just think about it. As I have already told you, I got into the Castle by letting myself be captured—quite deliberately. To do something that dangerous I must have had a really important objective. In fact, I must have known not only where the Necklace was hidden but also that I should be able to get at it from where I was certain to finish up."

Her cousin's eyes widened and his jaw hung open.

"You don't mean—?"

"Precisely." She rippled the Necklace with her hand so that it burned even more scintillatingly, and then hid its glories once more with her kerchief. "In the dungeon."

"So," Simon prompted, "by walking into a trap you were sure of getting the cheese."

"Except that I am not a mouse." She flashed him a smile.

"Yes, I knew that my father had hidden it in the dungeon. On his deathbed he told my mother exactly where. It was under a small flagstone in one corner. He put it there because he thought that the dungeon would be the one part of the Castle where no one would ever go, because most people think of dungeons as being totally outmoded and useless." She made a wry face. "That is, most civilized people do. But nowadays the Germans have some rather oldfashioned ideas."

"Tyranny is the oldest form of government," Simon observed. "That it happens to be one of the newest as well, merely brings it up to date and sets us all back a few centuries."

"But," argued Leopold, "how did you think you were going to get out again?"

"Oh, I would have got out even if you had not come after me," she stated airily.

"Really? And how did your clever little mind tell you you were going to accomplish that?"

She shrugged.

"I am a woman. The Kommandant there was a man." Her sophistication had a touch of malice. "He had already made that fact quite clear to me. What is more, he was not only a man but a snob. Oh yes, I should have got out all right."

"You would have degraded yourself and our family?" Leopold's face was a study.

"In England they call it 'letting down the side,'" Simon drawled. "That's because everything is a sport there. But you know, you really were being a bit scatterbrained."

Her look was defiant.

"Why? I tell you, I should have got out."

"Yes, dear old Countess and *femme fatale*," responded the Saint affably. "And Leopold and I might have got in—and stayed in. There'd be no point in *our* trying to seduce the Kommandant . . . although I must admit you never know with Prussian military types. It's probably all that leather and boots that gets them."

Frankie was suddenly subdued.

"I'm sorry. I never thought of that," she said in a small voice.

"That's what I mean," grumbled Leopold. "You never do think of anyone else."

Her eyes were moist and her lips trembled. All at once she had ceased being a poised young woman and was a girl.

"You know that's not true. Everything I did was for the sake of our family and our country."

"In that case," Simon put in, "it's about time you took a day off from being the keeper of the Hapsburg Necklace."

"What do you mean? Are you just being rude?"

"Not at all," said the Saint. "I'm being very polite—even complimentary. You'd make a terrific woman."

Frankie blushed warmly and was momentarily silenced. Leopold, on the other hand, was anything but at a loss for words.

"You are just making things worse," he snapped at the Saint.

Simon's brows lifted.

"By encouraging her to be a woman instead of a Guardian Angel? Isn't that what you would like?"

The other was becoming irascible again.

"That is none of your business. Frankie has been incredibly foolish, but what she does in her private life is her affair, or at least only the concern of our family. We do not permit strangers to intrude into our business."

The Saint was amused by Leopold's turnabout.

"Perhaps, dear old chap, that's what's been your trouble. With a good manager, you and Frankie might make the big leagues, but on your own you'll never sell yourselves. Puppet shows are out these days."

Although he was smiling, there was a hint of steel in his blue eyes.

This time it was Frankie who was the peacemaker.

"Come on, you two," she said soothingly, suddenly becoming very adult in her manner. "There's no point in our quarrelling. We have been through too much together." She turned to the Saint. "What do you think we are supposed to do now?"

"I'll go and ask Anton," he said. "Max must have given him instructions for us. Anyway, we need a good night's sleep. I for one won't mind bunking down here, then . . ."

He was interrupted by the sound of a motor. The headlights of a car raked the cabin as it came up the rutted path through the woods.

"This must be Max now," Frankie said with relief.

The Saint looked thoughtful.

"I wonder how he knew we were back? There's no telephone here, I presume, and smoke signals don't work at night."

"But naturally, he has simply come to see if we are back yet." Leopold sounded slightly impatient.

"Hold it," said the Saint sharply. "I don't think it's—"

Before he could finish his sentence the door was flung open from outside and two figures stepped into the room.

They were an incongruous pair, almost like a music hall turn: one large, one small, and both in ballooning raincoats.

"*Achtung!*" the small one said, and his gun lent authority to his words.

"*Kommt Zeit, kommt Rat,*" murmured the Saint, making a bilingual pun which he could only hope some bilingual reader would appreciate.

4

"Raise your hands, all of you," ordered the Rat in a flat business-like voice.

They did as they were told. The Saint was definitely annoyed. Even when it is a matter of life or death, standing with one's arms above one's head makes a man feel undignified. The Saint did not like the feeling. On the other hand, he was sure he wouldn't like the feeling of being dead, and just at the moment there was no other choice open to him.

Leopold's mouth was twitching as he gazed at the two men, hatred in his eyes. Frankie was calm, but her strained white face betrayed how desperate she was.

"Which of you has the Necklace?" inquired the Rat. He looked at Frankie. "Is it you, Frau Gräfin?"

She shook her head.

"We did not get it." Her lips were stiff.

"Well, we need not waste any more time," said the Rat. "There is one certain way of finding out. Strip, all of you!"

Leopold's eyes blazed as he took a step forward in spite of the gun trained unwaveringly at him.

"I will kill you for this," he said furiously.

"You will be lucky to stay alive very much longer, Herr Graf, if you go on behaving this way." The Rat's tone was infinitely sinister. "But perhaps we can save us all some trouble." He turned his gun on Frankie. Behind him the Gorilla stood with his pistol at the ready. "Come here please, Frau Gräfin."

Frankie stepped forward haltingly. She cast her eyes around desperately, as if looking for some escape from a hopeless situation.

Suddenly the Rat reached out and tore the shawl from her shoulders, pulling the top part of her blouse with it. Frankie's flesh gleamed like satin, and the Necklace rested on the soft cushion of her breast. For some reason, perhaps because of his heightened sensibilities, the Saint thought it looked more alive than ever.

"Ah," approved the Rat, "that is better." He turned to the Gorilla. "Keep them covered."

He stepped around Frankie and unfastened the Necklace, his fingers caressing her bare shoulders as he did so. She shivered and her face expressed her repugnance. The Rat held the

Necklace up so it splintered the light into a myriad different colours.

"*Wunderschön!*" he breathed. "It would be worth killing an army to get this." He turned to the Saint. "And thanks to you, *mein Herr*, we have got it without any bloodshed at all."

Simon's face was inscrutable.

"It strikes me," he remarked, "that you know a surprising amount for someone who just dropped in to pass the time of day, or night rather."

The Rat ignored his comment.

"Search the other," he commanded his mate as he stepped up to the Saint and frisked him swiftly, removing Simon's gun in the process.

The Gorilla did the same with Leopold. The Rat stepped to one side of the open door.

"We are leaving you now, but first we must tie you up." Turning to his companion, "Go fetch the rope," he said in German.

Suddenly the kitchen door opened and Anton entered.

The Gorilla's reaction was automatic. He did not even wait to think or see who it was. His gun spat once. The old man-servant slumped to the floor, an astonished expression on his face.

Then Leopold made his heroic move, which is something only heroes should attempt. He rushed blindly towards the Gorilla whose gun spoke again. Leopold stopped in his tracks, clutching his shoulder from which blood was beginning to seep.

Frankie gasped, and ran to him.

"Leopold, my darling!" she sobbed. She turned to the Gorilla. "You scum! You do not deserve to live!"

The Rat answered her. His smile was evil as he swung the Necklace tauntingly in front of her.

"And you, *Gnädiges Fräulein*, are lucky to be left alive." He spoke to the Gorilla out of the corner of his mouth: "Get the rope, I said."

"Why not just kill them?" grumbled the Gorilla. "They know too much anyway. And I know how I would like to do it to that other one."

"You are a fool," said the Rat contemptuously. "What he did to you was a proper punishment for your own stupidity. I order you to stop thinking about revenge and try to learn a lesson from it. The Boss said no killing, and now you have killed a man. Because of you we are already in deep trouble. Go get the rope, I am telling you."

Simon saw that the time had come for someone to take action. There was, of course, only one person capable of taking it: himself. Yet for reasons of his own that was the one thing he did not wish to do at that particular moment, and these reasons were totally unconnected with the fact that the odds were stacked so steeply against him. Nevertheless, it was a situation where discretion was the better part of valour, since the Rat had him well covered with his gun.

He therefore relaxed and lounged against the table while the Gorilla went out and quickly returned with a coil of cord, with which he set about tying up the Saint and his party. Simon submitted co-operatively to having his wrists bound, but was ready for the blow that the Gorilla launched at his face directly that was done, and ducked it easily, but could not keep his balance in evading the crotch kick that followed, and fell sideways.

"*Halt!*" commanded the Rat sharply, as the Gorilla's foot drew back for another kick. "You tie them up, nothing more. And you"—the muzzle of his gun fanned over his captives— "will not resist, unless you want to be painfully wounded."

The Gorilla muttered sulkily but got on with his job, and it was not long before the Saint, Leopold and Frankie were tightly trussed. Leopold's face turned dark red when the Gorilla leeringly gave Frankie some special pawing in the process, but his anger had to remain pent up. The Rat's gun saw to that. Frankie remained icily unmoved, and her eyes and expression showed scorn for his crudeness.

"There we are," said the Rat finally. "It would have been easier to kill you but we have our orders." He smiled cruelly at Simon. "And in your case, Mr. Templar, you are fortunate that I have had to restrain my associate in order to complete his punishment, not out of pity for you. But perhaps another time it will be different."

"Bless your tender heart, old fruit," drawled the Saint. "Any time you like. But I should warn you that I very seldom get killed—it's usually the other chap. I'd love to play some more games with your little friend. I think he needs to brush up on his knots, and we could do some practising on his neck."

The Rat's only response was to coldly motion with his gun for the Gorilla to precede him through the door into the darkness. The Gorilla swung a final kick at the Saint as he went, but Simon twisted away from it and sustained nothing worse than a brutal pain in his thigh. Then the Rat's gun itself peremptorily drove the Gorilla on his way, and the Rat followed. A few moments later the car starter hummed, and the engine burst into life. There was a clash of gears as it tore off down the bumpy lane, its headlights weaving wildly as it went.

"You gave up very easily," Leopold sneered. "Simon Templar, the Saint, the great champion—where was he?"

The Saint declined to take umbrage.

"He who lets them get away, gets his chance another day, as the Bard says. One can be brave and sensible at the same time. The Rat could have deaded me with one shot if I'd tried anything."

Leopold snorted. Frankie shot Simon a curious look but remained neutral.

"What do we do now?" she asked. "We could stay here for days, unless Max comes to find out what has happened to us."

"Cheer up, me hearties, all is not lost!" said the Saint jovially. "You are about to witness a marvel of escapology performed by none other than Simon H. Templar. The H stands for Houdini, of course. He was my aunt on my mother's side.

That was his greatest trick. But he taught me one or two others."

As he spoke, the Saint was flexing his arms.

"The secret is to keep your wrists edgeways-on while they're being tied. This gives the rope the greatest possible circumference to go around. Then when you turn them flat-to-flat, you get quite a bit of slack. Work that all to one side, and the loop may be big enough to pull one hand through. Of course it doesn't work if you're unconscious while they're tying you. But once you've done that, it's all downhill."

And suddenly his left hand came from behind his back, free and unencumbered, to give his audience a triumphantly mocking salute.

"Then," the Saint went on, as he shook the cords off his other hand and bent over to untie his ankles, "the rest is quite easy."

A minute or two later he kicked off the bonds and set about releasing Frankie.

The girl sat up and rubbed her wrists and ankles.

"I've gone all numb," she said.

"Don't worry," the Saint told her. "It always happens in cases of unrequited love. Feeling will come back soon, but you may get pins and needles for a while, as the seamstress said to the Bishop."

He stepped over to Leopold, who still lay bound and glaring at him.

"How would it be, old son, if we left you here as a corpus delicti? We ought to have some evidence that a crime has been committed. I mean mayhem as well as murder."

"You forget he is wounded," Frankie protested. "Set him free at once without making any more of your silly jokes."

"I'm sorry," Simon said humbly. "Being such a silly fellow, I suppose they come naturally."

He knelt down and began untying Leopold, and then helped the young man to a chair. Frankie came over and cradled Leopold's head on her shoulder. The young man looked quite pleased with life at the moment. He closed his eyes and a rather smug expression spread over his face.

"If you two were in a Victorian painting," Simon observed, "it would be entitled *The Prodigal's Return, or True Love Discovered.*"

Frankie flashed him a scathing glance.

"Even when poor Leopold may be dying and Anton is dead you try to turn everything into a joke. Have you no heart?"

The Saint stepped over to Anton, knelt down and felt the old servant's pulse.

"It's no joke about him," he said sombrely. "He must have died instantly. That trigger-happy gorilla must have thought the old boy was coming to our rescue. That's the trouble with these amateur hatchet men, or torpedoes as they're called in America. They often shoot first and hang later. I find I like that pair less and less every time I meet them. Perhaps we'll see to it that the next time is the last," he added grimly.

He crossed over to examine Leopold's shoulder.

"Not fatal," he announced shortly. "Luckily the bullet went clean through, and you don't have any vital organs up there unless you're built most peculiarly." He turned to Frankie. "I hate to ask you, but do you have any more underwear to spare? I mean, you must be getting down to bare essentials. But if you had a piece of . . . er . . . something . . . ?"

Frankie tore a strip off her last petticoat and tried ineffectually to bind up Leopold's wound. The boy gave a yelp of pain, and Frankie turned pleadingly back to Simon.

"All right," said the Saint easily. "Let Matron do it. In the Regiment they used to call me Florence the Nightlight, and strong soldiers wept in gratitude for my tender ministrations. At least, I think that's what they were crying about. Of course, they might have just been biting on an onion. They did that a lot in those days."

As he chatted nonsensically the Saint was efficiently and swiftly binding up Leopold's shoulder.

"There you are, sonny boy," he said when he had finished, "that'll do for the time being. See your local doctor when you get home and just remember to use your other arm when swinging from trees or hugging your girlfriend—or both. I'd put it in a sling but I don't think we can ask Frankie for any more sacrifices."

The young man sat up straight.

"You let them get away," he said uncompromisingly.

"I wasn't exactly in a position to stop them. I mean, I could have invited them to stop and play spelling games, but somehow I don't think they were in the mood."

"You don't seem to care at all that they've taken the Necklace," said Frankie acidly.

The Saint massaged his chafed wrists.

"My dear," he said blandly, "I would even have held the door open for them. We're well rid of them—and it."

VI

How Max received the news, and the Saint went for a climb

1

"You would have done *what?*" exploded Leopold.

"Escorted them out," Simon repeated. "Very politely. If they'd offered me a tip, I'd have taken it."

Frankie's incredulity was no less violent.

"You can't mean it, Simon!"

"I do, you know. They were very naughty boys, and they still had guns. I believe one should never get killed unless one has to—and then only as a last resort."

"But—but—but . . . they took the Necklace!"

"Ah yes, so they did," Simon agreed smoothly. "Well, perhaps it won't do them as much good as they think."

Frankie was taken aback.

"What do you mean?"

"Yes," Leopold said harshly. "Now they've got it, our whole cause is lost."

"You never know," Simon replied inscrutably. "The strangest things do happen, as the hen said when she hatched out an ostrich."

Frankie stamped her foot.

"Always you make a joke. Nothing is important to you. But that doesn't mean it isn't important to someone else. What about me? Is it nothing to you that I have betrayed my charge as Keeper of the Hapsburg Necklace?"

"To tell the truth, in words of one syllable," responded the Saint amiably—"No."

"You are impossible."

"Worse," Leopold amplified. "He is a coward."

The Saint was unmoved.

"That's right. I am. Only mugs get medals. Sensible men take good care to live to fight another day."

"Your reputation as a hero seems to have been easily earned," said Leopold sarcastically.

Still the Saint was not ruffled.

"Reputations don't matter. It is what a man knows about himself that counts."

"And does it mean nothing to you that Anton is dead?"

The Saint's eyes were expressionless although he smiled.

"I expect it means more to him. Presumably he was mixed up in this business of his own free will. I mean, he didn't have to work for Max, and he must have known that Max likes to live dangerously—and that goes for his associates, including me!"

Frankie shook her head.

"Sometimes I think you are just a machine."

The Saint shrugged.

"It's not such a bad thing to be if the machine is good enough. I'd like to be Rolls Phantom III Continental Touring Saloon with a V12 cylinder engine, 7,340 cc capacity. But right now I'd settle for almost anything on wheels in good running order."

"Simon, will you please stop! I'm not interested in your silly cars. I want to get my Necklace back."

The Saint moved towards the door.

"All right then, but aren't you a bit tired of hiking? It's a long way to walk."

"Where?" asked Leopold in perplexity.

"Back to Schloss Duppelstein."

"But if the Gestapo know about this place," Frankie argued, "Max must have been arrested, and—"

The Saint's voice was suddenly steely. "Look here, sweetheart, let's get something straight. You asked for my help. You got it—for better or for worse—until death do, etcetera. I'll get your Necklace back, but you must trust me."

"You did not try to stop them taking it," Leopold insisted.

"True," agreed the Saint. "But one of us might have been killed in the attempt, probably Frankie as she was the nearest. Look what happened to Anton. That reminds me. I suppose we'll have to notify the police eventually, so we'd better leave everything here just as it is."

"Since he was shot by the Gestapo," Leopold said, "why would the police be interested?"

Simon regarded him pityingly.

"You blessed innocent dimwit," he said. "Those two goons weren't the Gestapo. If they had been, and they were under orders not to shoot us out of hand, they'd at least have loaded us up and carted us off to one of their special rest homes. They wouldn't have left us here to get loose or be rescued by somebody."

The other two stared at him open-mouthed.

Leopold said: "Then you think—"

"That we were much too ready to buy that Gestapo story. There are still plenty of other villains in the world, plain ordinary commercial ones, and they haven't gone out of business just because Himmler came in. Obviously some of them, somehow, have got wind of you and your necklace, and they want it for purely mercenary reasons."

Frankie finally made up her mind.

"We're in your hands completely from now on, Simon."

"Okay," said the Saint. "Then may I go back to that car business I was talking about? I feel that there ought to be something here that Anton could have used if necessary, even if it isn't a Rolls."

It turned out to be a rather ancient Adler van, stabled in an open shed adjoining the cottage; but the key was trustfully in the ignition and the engine started after a few turns and ran purposefully if noisily.

Simon went back indoors and happily reported his find.

"We'll never catch our two playmates in it," he said, "but it should get us back to Max's. And that's an immediate priority—except to change these clothes, which the cops have probably had descriptions of by now."

"Max must have left something for us here," Leopold said, "in case we arrived wet from having to swim back across the river. Wait a minute. I'll go and look."

He went into the bedroom, and in a moment or so he returned bearing an armful of clothes.

"It's all right," he said, looking pleased with himself. "These are our own things. Frankie, there is an outfit in there for you."

"Good thinking, Leo," Simon approved generously. "So you hop in there, Frankie, and put on your party dress or whatever it is, while Leopold and I get changed here, and we'll be off. I must say I'm ready for some of the amenities of Max's château."

It did not take them long to get changed and packed into the one banquette seat of the shabby little van. The Saint drove, with Frankie pleasantly squeezed close to him in the middle. He had no doubt that a similar contact on her other side helped Leopold to endure the discomfort of his wound.

The rutted cart track by which the Rat and the Gorilla had reached the cottage, which was little more than a cleared space along which logs could be dragged in the work of forestation, eventually debouched on to a better secondary road. Banking on a usually reliable sense of direction, the Saint turned right, and in a few kilometres a signpost told him that they had rejoined the road by which Annellatt had brought him to the river crossing the previous evening.

Now the route back to Schloss Duppelstein was only a

problem for his memory, which in such situations had almost never failed him.

A growing sense of jubilation crept into him and began to dissipate his earlier fatigue.

"We're on our way again, boys and girls," he proclaimed. "And with one pain less in our necks. Maybe we're still unpopular on account of a slight argument at the border, but at least we know that we don't have the Gestapo to contend with. And anything less than that has got to be less formidable." A new-found optimism in him was effervescent and infectious. "Common or garden villains we can eat for canapés— and I'm sure Uncle Max has the underworld connections to put us on their tails!"

2

As it turned out, for the rest of the trip they were not even challenged. Either the alarum had been slow to disseminate from the border, or the local constabulary maintained reasonable working hours and were not about to go prowling after supper on the off-chance of running into some fugitives who should have had enough sense to be holed up somewhere for the night by that time.

When they reached Schloss Duppelstein, to their surprise the main gate of the Castle was open. It was usually locked at night. Max must have been expecting visitors, or perhaps someone had just left and the gates had not been closed after him. Maybe, because of Anton's absence, the routine of the Castle had been upset.

They walked across the courtyard without seeing any sign of life except a light high up in Max's study, another one in a ground-floor room, beneath the state rooms in the central block, and the lights of the great chandelier in the entrance hall.

The front door was unlocked, and as they entered the hall

they met the young footman Erich coming up from down-stairs, a pair of trousers hanging over his arm. His eyes widened when he saw the trio.

"*Ach, Frau Gräfin!*" he blurted. "Thank God you are back safely. The Herr Baron will be greatly relieved."

"Where is he, Erich?" Frankie asked as she swayed on her feet.

The footman stared at her with concern.

"Are you unwell, *Gnädigste?*"

"No, just tired. Very, very tired. But where is your Master?"

"He is upstairs in his study, *Gnädigste*. If you will allow me to go ahead I will tell him that you are here." He caught sight of the blood on Leopold's bandage. "The Herr Graf is injured!" he stammered.

"It is nothing, Erich," Leopold said, managing a smile. "An unfortunate accident. A mere pinprick."

Erich turned to Simon.

"And you, *mein Herr,* are you all right?" he asked in heavily accented English.

"Right as rain, whatever that means," replied Simon breezily. "But we could do with a good stiff drink and then bed."

"Ach, yes sir," said Erich. "Unfortunately Anton is away tonight, but I will get you something right away. Would you care to go into the library? There is a fire there still and I have not yet locked up for the night."

"That's true enough," said the Saint. "The alarm must be switched off or we couldn't have got in. By the way, why were the front gates open?"

"Anton usually sees to that, sir. I was going to attend to it, but I am new here and not very used to the routine." He fluttered his hands apologetically. "There is so much to do. Also the Master had visitors late tonight. I was about to put these away," he indicated the trousers on his arm, "and when I had done so I was going to lock the place up and switch on the alarm."

"Right," said the Saint. "We'll go into the library if you will tell the Baron that we're back." He was careful to conform with Annellatt's fictitious local identity. "But be a good chap, and don't forget the drink when you return—or perhaps even before you go!"

"Certainly, sir," replied the young footman obsequiously.

It struck the Saint that Erich was the kind of man who enjoyed taking orders. It was more a German type than an Austrian, but then the Germans owned Austria now, so perhaps Erich would prosper.

The servant was saved from having to go upstairs by the sudden appearance of Max on the balcony which ran around the top of the hall.

"Who is it, Erich?" he called. "Who are you talking to?"

"It's only us chickens," Simon called back.

For a long moment Max remained utterly still. Then he let out a mild oath and came hurrying downstairs.

"Frankie!" he cried, and caught her in an avuncular embrace.

She rested her head on his shoulder, too weary to say anything. Max looked past her at Leopold.

"What is that blood? Are you badly injured? What has happened?" He turned to the Saint. "Are you all right?" he asked anxiously.

The Saint grinned back at him.

"I'm suffering from acute thirst." He looked at the footman pointedly. "I think Erich was about to end the drought. Shall we go into the library and talk? I'm afraid we do have some bad news for you, about someone we had to leave behind."

Max's eyes widened as Erich hurried off towards the pantry.

"Who is that?" he asked when the servant was out of earshot.

"Anton is dead."

"Good God, who killed him?"

"How clever of you to know he was killed," Simon re-

marked. "But, you're right. It wasn't a heart attack, not even
a seizure. And he didn't die of old age. He was killed by one
of Frankie's kidnappers, the nasty little twerp who looks like a
rat."

"Come, we will go into the library," said Max. "You must
all be dead with tiredness."

He led the way helping Frankie along, and the Saint put
out a hand to steady Leopold as they followed.

As Erich had said, a fire was still burning in the book-lined
room. Max threw on a log and busied himself with stirring
up a blaze. Frankie sank into a leather-upholstered armchair.
Leopold collapsed full length on a sofa. The Saint sat easily
on an elegant gilded chair.

Max turned and faced them.

"My friends," he said. "I am only thankful to have you
back. For me it is unimportant whether or not you managed
to get the Necklace. I should never have allowed you to go,
and if you had been captured or killed I should have felt
guilty for the rest of my life. As it is, poor Anton . . ."

"We got the Necklace all right," Simon told him. "That is,
Frankie did."

Leopold groaned. Frankie lay back quite still and silent in
her chair, her eyes closed.

"*Gott im Himmel!*" Annellatt's voice almost cracked. "The
Necklace too! It is almost too much to have you three back
safely, *and* the Necklace as well—"

"But unfortunately we haven't still got it," the Saint went
on. His voice was bland, almost conversational. He could
have been talking about the weather.

Max's face dropped dramatically.

"I don't understand."

"Just that those two Gestapo types took it away from us.
That's how Anton got killed. It was a very nasty case of
trigger-happiness. But it was not a Gestapo job."

Erich came into the room just then, bearing a silver tray on
which were a decanter and several glasses.

"Thank you, Erich," said Simon. "You are a ministering angel. Remind me to leave a halo under your pillow when I go."

The servant placed the tray on a table, bowed impassively, and left the room. Max walked over and started pouring out the drinks.

"What did you mean by that?" he demanded. "About the Gestapo?"

With a glass in his hand, Simon settled down to recap the whole story, as briefly as he could without leaving anything important out. He wanted to be sure that Max got the picture exactly as he saw it himself.

Annellatt's bright brown eyes concentrated raptly on his face throughout the recital.

"And so," Simon concluded, "the Gestapo might or might not take an interest in that little scuffle I got into at the border, but they aren't after us for the Necklace—which is good for us. On the other hand, what's bad is that we haven't a clue where to start looking for this mob that's hijacked it. Unless your 'connections' can get a line on them."

Annellatt's knitted brows only expressed the intensity of his concentration.

"That may be easier than you think," he said. "You three have done more than your share. Now, when I have put a proper dressing on poor Leopold's wound—I am quite qualified to do it, without sending for a doctor who might ask embarrassing questions—you should all get some rest, while I go to work. Tomorrow I may have a surprise for you."

3

The Saint did not go to sleep.

He did not even get undressed, although he drank the hot chocolate from the Thermos which Erich had thoughtfully placed on his bedside table.

He stood by the window of his room in the central block of the Castle on the floor above the state rooms, and gazed out over the moon-washed roofs of the Castle. It was a romantic sight. So it must have looked on moonlit nights for centuries to people long dead and gone. But the Saint was not concerned with the past. It was the urgent present which occupied his mind.

He looked across to where the light still gleamed from Max's study window. For the Saint it illuminated one inescapable fact.

The time had come for action. The final drama was about to be played out. But first he must go and see Max. By himself. That enigmatic man with the charm which he could turn on and off at will, and a mind as calculating as a machine, yet filled with warmth and humour, must be told certain facts. And he must be informed of them without delay, late though the hour was. Otherwise the Hapsburg Necklace might be lost to them for ever.

The Saint slipped out of his room and down the passage to the balcony round the top of the main hall. Here the lights had been extinguished, but the moon broke through the slats of the shutters to illuminate portions of the black and white marble floor of the hall below him.

The Saint moved like a wraith in the shadows. It was as if he had become a shade himself. Anyone standing in the hall would neither have seen nor heard him. On the far side he tried the door leading to the other rooms of the central block on that floor, and from thence to Max's wing. It was locked. The Saint had suspected it might be. Max was the sort of man who would ensure total privacy for himself.

Simon took out of his pocket a piece of wire which he usually kept in his suitcase ready for emergencies, and picked the lock. It was to no avail. The door was barred or bolted on the other side, and the hinges were on that side too.

Well, Max was going to have a visitor tonight whether he liked it or not. The Saint was determined on that. There was too much at stake to allow Max the perfect seclusion he desired. There was only one snag. All normal methods of getting to Max's study were barred and the entire ground floor of the central block, as Anton had explained to him, was wired with burglar alarms, including the inside doorways leading from the main hall to the state rooms. Thus all communication with the wings was prevented at that level.

On the floor where he was there were no burglar alarms, and had not the door leading to Max's wing been barred, he could have walked straight through and along to Max's study. He could, of course, go around to the other side of the balcony and into the wing which housed Frankie and Leopold, for this must surely be open. Then he could make his way to the ground floor and unbolt a door into the courtyard. But he did not know the set-up in that part of the Castle. That wing could be bristling with henchmen and servants—and no one must be allowed to get in the way of his private session with Max that night.

But it rather looked as if someone did mean to interfere. The door leading to the stairway from the main hall to the rooms below the state apartments suddenly opened, and the black and white flagstones of the great hall far below were brightly lit up by a wedge of electric light as someone came through that door into the hall. It was Erich. The Saint could not see him but he heard his voice calling out some instruction to another person still in the basement. Then Erich began to mount the stairs, curiously without turning on the lights and treading lightly.

There was nothing for it but to beat a retreat unless Simon was willing to be involved in a tiresome extempore explanation of why he himself was coming down the stairs. The Saint did not want any such encounter. For personal reasons he wanted his visit to Max to be completely private.

He slipped noiselessly back round the balcony and into his room. He heard Erich's footsteps coming stealthily nearer, and then they stopped outside his door.

The situation was piquant enough to be just to the Saint's liking. He figured that for some reason Erich apparently was about to enter his room, presuming that by now the Saint was fast asleep. If he found the Saint awake he would probably make some excuse and depart, possibly taking with him the Saint's shoes to polish, or some article of clothing for pressing.

Indulging himself, the Saint gave vent to a loud snore. There was nothing he would have liked better than to catch Erich sneaking into his room and surprise him by jumping out of the dark and saying "Boo!" He could picture the astonishment, dismay, fright, and total incomprehension on the man's face.

The door slowly opened, inch by inch. This time the Saint added a grace note to his snore. It was a truly operatic production and he was pleased with it.

But surprisingly Erich did not open the door further. Instead, Simon could see in the moonlight the manservant's arm curl silently around the door and equally silently remove the key from the lock.

It took a lot to confuse the Saint, but for a moment he was completely flummoxed. Then the door closed without a sound. A moment later there was a click as the lock turned, and there was a grating noise, slight but unmistakable, as the key was withdrawn.

The Saint realised that for some reason Erich had made him a prisoner. He would probably come back in the morning, unlock the door, and wake Simon just as if nothing had happened. The thought amused Simon.

But the fact that he had been barred from wandering spelled out clearly that something was going on in the Castle that visitors must not know about. Well, Erich and any of his pals could play their games and he could play his. But it was now imperative that he get to Max as quickly as possible.

He went to the window and leaned out. The height from the courtyard had looked alarming enough in daylight, but at thing about it: Erich and his colleagues would never think that the Saint would leave his room by such a dangerous route.

Now he was reminded that one happening after another had bereft him of conventional fire-power. But in the bottom of his suitcase, still untouched, was the switch knife which he had taken from the Gorilla in Vienna and kept as a souvenir of that encounter. As he slipped it into his hip pocket, he felt a surge of invincible excitement that had its source in days of youthful recklessness that he had sometimes almost forgotten.

The thought that he might not survive such a vertiginous descent did not bother him at all. His theory had always been that his time would come when it did, and that certainly was not yet. He expected to go on operating on this theory for many years to come. It had got him out of scrapes which would not only have daunted others but which would have been lethal to them as well. "High ho, the long drop O," he sung gently to himself as he swung one leg over the window-sill and prepared to climb down the face of the building to the courtyard below.

It was going to be a difficult, almost impossible journey. His room was at a corner of the central portion of the Castle, which meant that he did not have the aid of the colonnaded balconies that adorned the wings. Once on the ground, it would be relatively easy for him to break into the wing which housed Max's study, since this was not equipped with burglar alarms. But first he had to get down to the courtyard.

Although most of his enemies, and indeed the majority of his friends too, would not credit it, the Saint was subject to human failings, including the very natural protective fear of heights which is instilled into humans to keep them from thinking they are mountain goats. On the other hand, his whole training had been to neutralise these weaknesses. In dealing with heights, therefore, he was as cautious as the best mountain climber, but he had long ago evolved a system of overcoming vertigo and muscle-freezing panic. It was very simple. He just pretended that the height on which he stood was two feet off the ground and told himself firmly that he could therefore not possibly be hurt if he fell. It was a psychological trick, deliberately practised to fool himself, but it worked.

He leaned now over the cobblestone courtyard, casually holding on with one hand to the jamb of the window, and examined the face of the building. He might have been surveying the North Face of the Eiger, looking for footholds preparatory to an organised climb complete with ropes, crampons, ice axes and all the necessary equipment. But in this case he had nothing to rely on except his own strength, agility and coolness.

The climb at first sight appeared totally impossible, even for him. His idea had been to get on to the roof and walk across to a point above Max's window, and then climb down. But he could see now that this scheme was not feasible. There was simply no surface between him and the roof which would give the necessary holds. Nor was there anything which would provide an opportunity for him to work his way sideways along the front of the building to the wing. The stuccoed plaster on either side of his window was as smooth as a board, and the neighbouring windows were too far away for him to swing across to, even if he cared to take such a potentially lethal risk.

On the other hand, perhaps the Saint's greatest asset was his conviction that no problem was unsolvable, if you approached it with an open mind. He had to reach Max's wing somehow, and if he could not do it by climbing upwards, then the feat might be accomplished by making a descent.

As in most Renaissance buildings, the State Apartments were on the floor above the ground floor and below the one on which the Saint was. The windows of these large rooms opened on to an ornamental stone ledge above the top of the ground floor which on the outside was "rusticated" with plaster imitation slabs of stone. The tops of these state room windows were covered with a jutting pediment of stone. If he could drop on to the one below him, he could climb down on to the windowsill and then simply work his way down the rusticated stonework of the ground floor to the courtyard. Then he could walk across to Max's wing and climb up the outside of it to the canopied verandah. From the roof of this it would be a relatively easy climb to Max's study.

Some might have considered that only a superb gymnast with a lunatic mind could seriously consider this enterprise. The Saint would have laughed and agreed with them. But without further hesitation, he gripped the windowsill with both hands and gently lowered himself downwards, singing "Onward, Christian Soldiers" in a low voice as he did so. It was not the most appropriate of songs but it had a strong vigorous tune and remembering the words kept his mind occupied and away from thoughts of the void below. When his arms were fully extended he let himself drop.

4

His descent was short and sharp and he landed on the ledge on top of the window underneath. The drop had to be completely accurate, for the stone pediment was not more than about a foot wide and if his body had swayed outwards in landing he would have crashed backwards to the courtyard below. As it was, in order to save himself from the natural inclination to teeter, and to keep his body pressed against the face of the building, he had to use every ounce of his determination, will-power and muscular strength.

With infinite caution, and this time humming "Rock of Ages" by way of a change, he turned around and lowered his body to a sitting position on the ledge.

So far so good, but his difficulties were not yet over. He had to get down to the windowsill some twelve feet below, and this sill sloped slightly outwards to cast rain off into the courtyard below. That slight declivity might also throw a Saint on to the cobblestones—and the sill was high enough to make that a formidable fall.

One thing was certain. He could not go back. He must go on, even if it meant purposefully dropping the rest of the way on to the cobblestones. But that might easily result in a broken leg or at least a sprained ankle—and possibly even in death if the drop were miscalculated. The Saint felt very strongly that death would curtail his activities, and there were certain of them he was not yet ready to give up.

Then he remembered that the window below him was in two sections: a relatively small area of glass permanently fixed at the top above a transverse wooden lintel, and below this two large window sections which opened outward on hinges like doors. If he could break part of the top section without setting off an alarm, he could get an arm through it and lever himself down on to the sill.

Thought was followed by immediate action. Taking off his shoes he tied the laces together. Then he hung the shoes around his neck. He manoeuvred himself so that once more he faced inwards, and then lowered his body off the ledge slightly to one side of the window.

He was now hanging so that he faced the window. As carelessly as if it were the most everyday thing in the world the Saint let go with one hand. Then, taking the shoes from around his neck, he used one of them to break one of the small panes in the top part of the window. A few splinters fell to the cobblestones but most of the glass dropped inside, between the glass panel below and the interior curtains. To the Saint the noise seemed vastly magnified, but his cool mind told him that unless somebody had been in the room or the courtyard no one would have heard it. He cleared the remaining splinters of glass from the wooden frame with his shoe, and then hung the pair of them back round his neck. He thrust his arm through the hole he had made and let go of the pediment above with his other hand, thus allowing his body to swing downwards until his feet touched the sill.

He was now able to turn his body so that he was half facing outward. At this point he realised that the "rustication" was not going to do him any good—on his way down at any rate. It might be of help in climbing the face of Max's wing, but there was no way in which he could get his feet off the ledge and into the crevices between the fake stone slabs below. He considered for a long moment what he should do and finally decided that there was nothing for it but to drop the remaining distance to the courtyard below. He had, after all, reached a point where he was standing only a floor above the ground, and whereas a fall backwards off the sill would have proved damaging or even fatal, a deliberate drop for a man of the Saint's athletic prowess was quite feasible. He might end up with a few bruises but it was unlikely that he would suffer any more grievous harm.

He twisted himself so that his feet faced outward on the sill. Then he dropped his shoes on to the cobblestones. Finally, he let go of the lintel above his head.

For a moment he balanced, poised on the windowsill like a huge bird ready for flight. Then he sank to a sitting position, reducing by that much the height from which he had to fall, and pushed himself off.

The drop was a bone-shaking one, to put it mildly, but it was no worse than a parachute landing, of which he had done a few. As his feet touched the ground he relaxed his knees and body-rolled across the pavement. Of course, the cobblestones were distinctly unresilient cushions to land on, and had it been anyone else who was landing on them that person might have been quite severely hurt. But the Saint's muscles, fitness and agility allowed him to get away with it.

He picked himself up off the stones and straightened his clothing.

"Well, well, well," he remarked to himself inaudibly.

"What a carry on. I must remember to bring a rope ladder next time I go for a country visit."

It was his own way of congratulating himself on the successful conclusion of his descent. It might of course have been more seemly if someone else had done it, but there was no one else around to perform that service. And in its own way, perhaps, that lack of an audience was itself a compensation.

Simon took the shoes from around his neck, untied the laces, and put them back on. Then he surveyed the side of the wing beneath the light of Max's study.

With any luck he should not have to do any more climbing. It was, after all, only the central block of the Castle, housing the state rooms and its treasures, that was fitted with a burglar alarm system. If he could gain entrance through a ground-floor window of the wing, therefore, there would be little risk of rousing anyone at this time of night, or rather morning, and he could simply walk upstairs to Max's study, since the only doors in the wing with burglar alarms were those leading from it to the state rooms.

Using his knife, the Saint slipped the catch of a ground-floor sash window. He opened the window and quickly dealt with the shutters inside. Luckily for him they were only secured by a catch and not a bar. Obviously Max was not worried about burglars in that part of the building. There was no reason why he should be. A burglar would have to gain entrance to the courtyard before arriving where the Saint was, something which would be none too easy after the gates had been locked for the night. Only Annellatt's obsession with his own security made a burglar alarm even remotely necessary there.

Simon found himself in a small room. As far as he could see in the dark it was a sort of office. He did not bother to investigate, and went straight to the door opposite and through it into what proved to be a long passage. At the end of this a flight of stairs led upwards, and these he took on soundless tiptoes.

On the landing at the top of the stairs two flights up the light from under the door of Max's study shone like a beacon. Swiftly Simon crossed over to it and with infinite gentleness turned the handle of the door and pushed it open.

Max was sitting behind a large desk. He looked up in slack-jawed startlement as the Saint entered.

On the blotter in front of him crouched Thai, gazing at the Hapsburg Necklace with unwinking eyes.

VII

How Thai did his bit, and sundry other characters got their deserts

1

Max recovered himself in a moment and put down the jeweller's eyeglass with which he had been examining the Necklace. Master and cat looked at Simon steadily.

"Come in, my friend," Max said genially. "As you can see, we have got the Necklace back."

Simon sauntered over and sat down in a chair opposite the desk. Though his attitude was relaxed, his eyes were on the alert in case the Austrian made a move to get a gun out of a drawer.

"I think, old fruit, you and I had better have a talk," he said pleasantly.

Max's eyebrows rose.

"Ach, but certainly. What do you wish to talk to me about?"

His hand caressed the back of Thai's neck. The cat gave Simon a sardonic look.

"Well, to begin with," said the Saint, "let's clear up one thing. Are you working for yourself or the Germans?"

"I do not know why you should ask. You and I are on the same side. We have been all along."

Simon shook his head. "No, we haven't. You've tried to bamboozle me right from the beginning. I let you think you'd succeeded because I was curious to find out what you were up to."

Max leaned back in his chair. His eyes did not waver. The cat moved over and climbed on his shoulder where he apparently went to sleep. But Thai had a strange quality of seeming to be dangerous even when at his mildest. It struck the Saint that this characteristic was shared by the cat's master.

"All right," said Max, "I am curious to find out where you get such absurd ideas. Let me hear some of your thoughts, wrong though they may be. When did you first begin to suspect me in your mistaken way?"

The Saint thought of the Rat and the Gorilla—and Anton lying dead on the floor of the hut. Max's undeniable charm concealed some very nasty secrets.

"I mistrusted you all along, but that didn't mean a thing. I mistrusted Frankie and Leopold as well to begin with. Of course, I should have rumbled it that night in Vienna, when you were so conveniently delayed and let me in to be banged on the head by those two thugs who were waiting for me in the garage. But I only thought of that later. No, I think I first began to suspect you when you were so cool about the intervention of the "Gestapo." Any ordinary person would have been scared reasonably spitless. But when I realised that the Rat and the Gorilla could be working for you, I knew you might be against Frankie also."

"I don't understand." Max sighed wearily. "Forgive me, but what reason had you for not believing that the thought of the Gestapo did not automatically terrify me?" Thai suddenly opened his eyes wide and gave the Saint a look which seemed to say "Answer that if you can!"

"I didn't believe it because it wasn't in character. An Austrian might have fallen for it, it was crazy enough to appeal to the Austrian mind. But to me it was completely phoney. I've been around, Max, and I know your type. A smart operator and manipulator, yes, but only when you have first chance at stacking the deck. Not the type who goes into anything with the odds against him, or when he runs the risk of getting personally and physically hurt."

Annellatt looked mildly offended.

"It's the sort of thing you do, Mr Templar."

The Saint could not help but admire his coolness. The Austrian was in a nasty spot but he might have been discussing the high price of coffee for all the tension that he showed.

"No one would ever accuse me of being your type," Simon said. "But to get back to you. Why didn't you just go to the police if you thought Frankie had been kidnapped? After all, she hadn't done anything illegal—if she really was the hereditary Keeper of the Necklace."

Max wagged his head patiently.

"In normal times, yes. But nowadays even the police are not entirely respectable. Don't forget that the Gestapo controls Vienna and its police and I am sure the Germans would not be willing to see the Necklace taken away, perhaps altogether out of their hands. My concern was only to help Frankie in what she thought was her duty."

The Saint shook his head.

"The Gestapo were never involved. The Rat and the Gorilla were not Gestapo, not even the Austrian branch. They were too inefficient for one thing." His voice was suddenly cold and his blue eyes grew icy. "You thought you were dealing with a foreigner who wouldn't understand the Austrian character. You thought I would buy your story that you just were in your quaint Austrian way trying to strike a blow against the invading tyrants." His tone grew even chillier. "You were not just unlucky, you picked on the wrong man. Most foreigners think that because the Austrians do crazy things they are all a bit mad. I happen to think that there are few races that are more sane. The Gemans live in a dream world and try to make it real. The Austrians live in a real world and only pretend to dream."

Max chuckled.

"That is a good epigram, but like all good epigrams it is as false as it is true. So now you have decided that I am a villain, and the men you have been fighting were in my employ. What, may I ask, could I have possibly have gained from such actions?"

"In Austria," said the Saint, "you have to be aware that one and one often make three. In this case the Rat and the Gorilla added up to a third person who controlled them, you. You stood to gain quite a lot and to lose nothing at all."

"Oh yes?" Max's eyes sparkled with interest. He actually seemed to be enjoying himself.

"Yes. You see, I remembered that when we met in your apartment Frankie told you I knew where the Necklace was. She merely meant that she had informed me that it was in Schloss Este, and she was about to explain this when Leopold interrupted and lost his temper. After that the whole thing got sidetracked, but you concluded that she had told me more than she had you. From that moment on, I became useful to you. So you had me slugged in the garage by your men, who were told to extort the information from me. If they got it, you'd be in the clear all along the line, for if I survived I'd think I'd been kidnapped by the Gestapo, and you would be free to double-cross Frankie at the most propitious moment."

"But why, may I ask, if I was working, as you say, against her, could I not have seized her in the first place and forced her to tell me everything I needed to know?"

"Because until you knew exactly where the Necklace was hidden, you didn't know if it might be impossible for anybody except Frankie herself to get at it."

"But then why would I let you join the party, to add another complication?" Max smiled disarmingly. "Even for an Austrian, is that not a bit exotic?"

"You wanted to keep all your options open, and you didn't let me join—Frankie stuck you with me. You had to accept me or have me bumped off, fast, to maintain your credibility, for you knew I was a dangerous customer to fool around with. You wanted to keep an eye on me. Also you decided I might be more useful alive than dead. You'd figured out another angle."

"What was that?" Max might have been listening with polite fascination to a tale Simon was inventing.

"It was that you might be able to get me to work for you."

"*Phantastisch!*" said Herr Annellatt.

Thai seemed to blink in sleepy agreement.

"Maybe. But it's all true."

Max's head moved in negation.

"It is a very interesting story, but you give yourself a little too much credit. After all, I am a wealthy man and I could employ any number of people to do the job of getting the Necklace. Why should I be so ready to engage you?"

"For two reasons. When you realised I didn't know exactly where the Necklace was hidden in the Castle, you figured that Frankie might trust me more than you. You've been up against that deadlock for months. Frankie would never tell you where it was. You thought I might perhaps get it out of her."

"Why you rather than me?"

The Saint smiled with shameless impudence.

"Possibly because I'm a more romantic type."

"And the second reason?"

"Because I am the Saint. You knew my reputation, and so do a lot of dreary policemen. You thought you could let me get the Necklace for you, and then steal it from me, and still throw me to the cops as the fall guy."

"And so I persuaded Frankie to run away to Hungary just to get you to go after her?" Max spoke drily.

"Not at all. You were genuinely surprised and upset by her going. So was I. It loused up both our plans completely. You had to improvise a new one in a hurry."

"And what was this new one?"

Max's voice was silky. Both he and Thai regarded Simon from between narrowed lids.

"I must say you kept your head. You had to act fast because Frankie was going into Gestapo territory, and if she got captured your chances of getting the Necklace would have been finished. That meant you had to work with me and against me at the same time, once I had volunteered to go and get her out."

"Surely all this is too clever, even for me," Max protested.

Simon's smile held genuine warmth.

"No, it's not too clever for you, nor for me. It's a pity we're on opposite sides. We have very much the same kind of brain. But perhaps it's inevitable that we should compete. There's only room for one at the top, and I have a big advantage over you."

"What is that?"

"I work on my own and do all my own dirty work. You have to rely on other people to do yours for you. That makes you as vulnerable as they are. For instance, your tame Rat made the mistake of addressing me by name, which he shouldn't have known unless he'd been told. That was another thing that helped to confirm my suspicion that those two nasties were hooked up with you."

Annellatt's mouth turned down at one corner.

"It cuts both ways. If you lose once you lose totally. I can lose a lot of times and still win in the end."

"In other words, your associates are expendable," said the Saint sardonically.

"Exactly."

"Like Anton." The Saint looked directly into Max's eyes.

For a moment Max's gaze flickered.

"Believe it or not, that was a mistake. He was only a servant. I never thought he would be in any danger. It made me very sad. He was such a nice man."

"He only made the mistake of working for you, in fact."

"Possibly. But I tell you, I am sorry about Anton." Max's voice became warm, almost caressing, as he leant forward across the desk. "I still think we might work together, my friend."

The Saint shook his head. "No dice. I don't change my habits so easily. But to get back to your cunning little scheme. It was pretty clever, I admit. You'd probably worked out a method of getting across the border a long time ago. In fact, you told me as much. The cleverness lay in incorporating these old plans with the new and in keeping out of the whole affair yourself."

"Explain yourself a bit further."

"On the surface you were helping us. But you arranged to have your men hijack the Necklace when we got back to the cabin. Though how they knew when we got back I still don't know. I suppose you just told them to check the cabin at regular intervals. Wouldn't it have been simpler if they'd waited for us there?"

Max flashed him a shrewd look.

"Were I the villain you think I am, I might not have wanted to run the risk of your seeing them or their car before you got settled in and relaxed."

The Saint nodded.

"That would add up, especially as you told Anton to hold us there until someone arrived." He looked at Max levelly. "You know, that Gorilla of yours really shouldn't be allowed out. Is he a dope addict or something? I mean, for anyone to be so slug-happy is plain ridiculous. He shot Anton without even looking to see who he was!"

"A very stupid man, almost an animal," agreed Max benignly. "Such people are dangerous, but they are also sometimes useful."

"You figured we'd never know he was working for you and would think that the Gestapo must somehow have got on to your plans. That's why you were able to welcome us back with such hospitality. Otherwise you would have made sure we were all killed, either in the cabin or somewhere along the line. Like me, you prefer to avoid complications whenever possible. It must have been a nasty shock when you found you were a candidate for a murder rap."

Max stiffened.

"I was a candidate for what?"

"A murder rap. It's American slang. It means you were responsible for Anton's death even though you didn't plan it, do it, or even want it."

"But how can that be?"

"I imagine Austrian law recognises some universal principles. Anyone who is an accessory to a crime must take the consequences as much as the person or persons who commit it. That makes you guilty."

Max leaned back in his chair and surveyed the Saint thoughtfully.

"You know," he said, "I like you. I like you very much. I don't know how old you are, but you look young enough to be the son I never had, and I am not all that old myself. If we had been on the same side, perhaps you might have inherited my . . . er . . . connections." He unleashed a smile. "But with regard to the Hapsburg Necklace—"

"That proves your guilt if nothing else," interrupted Simon.

Annellatt raised his shoulders.

"My lawyers would put up a good defence. You still don't really know how I got it."

"You could only have got it from the Rat or the Gorilla. That's another crime in this country, I'm sure. There must be a law against stealing national monuments."

Max's smirk was almost triumphant.

"Ah, but I did not steal anything of the kind."

"What do you mean? There it is." Simon pointed to the Necklace which glimmered in a heap of fire on the desk.

"Do you know anything about jewels?" Annellatt asked.

"Enough to get by."

Max picked up the Necklace from the desk and tossed it over to Simon.

"It's a fake," he said.

2

Simon caught the Necklace deftly.

It shimmered and glittered with a thousand facets of light. Reaching over, he picked up Max's jeweller's magnifying glass and examined it. He was expert enough to be able to confirm at once that Max was telling the truth. The feel of the gems, moreover, gave them away. They lacked the voltage quality of real stones. The fires, though beguiling to the eye, were as false as those created for the grates of luxury flats or for sinners by evangelical missionaries.

Again he was shaken but not rocked out of reason. In his life, anything could happen and often did. But there was always a good reason for even the most extraordinary occurrences.

The explanation behind this one was fairly easy to see. Frankie's father, grandfather, or one of her ancestors, must have had a duplicate made, perhaps with a view of selling the original secretly. Such a plot might have been a criminal conspiracy, but this did not make it any more improbable. To aristocrats, honour was all important, second only to exposed insolvency. If a distinguished bankruptcy could have been averted by the substitution of a string of baubles that would bedazzle anyone but a probing expert, what was the harm? Besides, the Necklace might even have been hocked with the connivance of the Austrian Government, to raise money for the State Treasury. Such things had been known to happen in the convolutions of Balkans economics.

On the other hand, the false necklace could have been made to safeguard the real one, for use as a decoy, red herring or other fraud to occupy the attentions of crooks, while the genuine one rested safely in secret custody.

In any case, the necklace he held in his hand was worthless to him, Max, Frankie, the Third Reich, or anyone else concerned with the value of the original. It was a beautiful piece of work and undoubtedly cost a tidy sum, but compared to the real thing it was only worth its weight in peanuts.

"You must be very disappointed," remarked Simon. "I mean, after all your hard work and the efforts of your bully boys, to end up with a pup must be disheartening to say the least. Oh, well, don't let it get you down. Every silver lining has a cloud, as my Aunt Agatha used to say about her rich fat husband."

Max smiled wryly. "You are an incredible man. We Austrians may make a joke about everything, but underneath we take it seriously. I believe you really do see everything as a joke."

"A very serious joke."

Annellatt sighed.

"What interests me very much now is where is the real Necklace?"

"Well, if it's not still at Schloss Este or some Swiss bank or other, I have a business pal who could find out who sold it to whom recently—if it was recently. I have just concluded a deal with him myself, and there isn't much that goes on above board or under the counter in the international diamond markets that he doesn't know about."

Max's eyes narrowed shrewdly. "Do you think Frankie knows?"

"Who knows? She might be trying to cover up some ancestral fiddling, for the honour of the family. Or she might be trying to outsmart all of us."

"We shall have to find out."

"I shall have to find out."

The set of Annellatt's head took a speculative slant.

"Does that mean you would consider working with me?"

"No more than I have already. We weren't made to be partners. We'd always be competing. Besides, as I've said before, I don't change my loyalties so easily."

"Neither do I. But my prime loyalty is to myself. Surely yours is too?"

"Not always. Believe it or not, I'm quite old-fashioned sometimes. I believe in honour and the code of a gentleman. I know it's a bit out of date but purely practically it does make civilisation work. I mean, even Hilter would find life easier if one could trust his word."

Max laughed, a trifle ruefully. "You mean you can't trust mine?"

"I haven't said that."

"Ah, but you have implied it. I have a feeling that if I were an Austrian aristocrat you would feel differently."

"I know a lot of aristocrats who are not gentlemen at all," smiled the Saint. "And conversely, I know a lot of gentlemen who are not aristocrats."

"But I am neither. I am an Austrian peasant who has made good, as you say in your language."

It was an extraordinary conversation, at such a time. But Simon had long since realised that Max Annellatt was no ordinary man, and he was intrigued enough to let the chat take its course.

"Good—or bad. It depends on which way you look at it."

"I am rich," Max said flatly. "That is always good for the person who is rich."

"Especially if he doesn't care what lengths he goes to to get richer," said the Saint, leaning back lazily.

Max's expression became serious.

"When I was a child, my father used to beat me regularly, either because I had been bad, or to keep me from being bad —but mostly because he was drunk." The smoke from his cigarette curled upwards, and suddenly there was a break in its smooth flow. "I have had a horror of violence ever since."

"That's why you ordered your men to grab me and work

me over, I suppose," said Simon sympathetically. "Presumably when they shot Leopold and when they killed Anton it was all in the spirit of fun."

Max shook his head.

"Anton's death was a mistake, and I am truly sorry for it. My men did not know he was in the cabin, and when he came in through the door suddenly, one of them shot him before he recognised him."

"That takes a load off my mind, if not off Anton's," said the Saint. "It's good to know you're really a nice chap at heart. But it must be an awful disappointment to you not to have got the Hapsburg Necklace."

Annellatt spread his hands all the way from his shoulders downwards.

"One cannot always win. There will be other times and other businesses. Besides, I may yet get the real Necklace."

"It's highly unlikely," the Saint assured him. "When the police hear about Anton and your other activities, you'll be lucky if you just spend the rest of your life in jail and not dead, if you will forgive an Irishism."

"We shall see about that. I have resources—some of them in other places than Austria."

"And this little shack—you could afford to just walk away from it?"

"As you know, it is not in my own name. And there is an enormous mortgage, at atrocious interest. I might be much better off without it."

The Saint felt himself quite irresistibly compelled to let Annellatt continue to entrench his theoretical position.

"I suppose you've got it all worked out, how we could carve the joint between us."

Max put all his considerable charm into a smile.

"I think, Simon," he said, "that this conversation—and this necklace—had better be a secret between us."

"Why?"

"Because it would do no good to tell anyone else and would probably be harmful."

"To you, yes. To be honest, it wouldn't bother me at all."

Annellatt's reaction was vehement.

"No, if Frankie knew of it, she might insist on going back to Schloss Este to look for the real one."

"And suppose she already knew?"

"Then we should have to find out what happened to it."

"With the help of some of your special operatives?" The Saint's voice was tinged with acid. "No, dear old fruit, I think we should have it out with Frankie and Leopold face to face. I suppose you've locked them in their rooms too?"

"No, the only one I was afraid of was you. They would not be likely to wander around the Castle after everyone had gone to bed. But you, Simon, you have a propensity for poking your nose into other people's business."

"So *that's* why you had me locked up for the night."

Annellatt's gesture was mildly apologetic.

"I wanted to make sure of not being disturbed while I examined the Necklace and arranged to have it transported away from the Schloss. There are people who are eagerly awaiting it, and until just before you made your rather dramatic entrance, I thought it was the real thing. Your door would have been unlocked and you would probably never have known anything about it. How did you get out, by the way?"

"I flew," Simon said with a perfectly straight face. "That's something about me you didn't know. I grow wings after dark. All right, so Frankie and Leopold are not locked in. Let's talk it over with them right now."

"I am ready."

"And how will you explain how the frontier guards knew that the false papers which we presented at the frontier—which you provided—were fakes, and they were waiting for them?"

"Only," Max said intelligently, "if there was a leak in my own organisation."

"Then you'd better start thinking about it," said the Saint.

Max stood up. He was still exercising all his usual charm of manner, but there was something suddenly remote about him and curiously forceful.

"You have not counted on one thing, while you are giving me orders."

"And that is?"

"I may not be as strong nor as brave as you. But I am just as clever and I never get into a situation that I can't get out of."

There was utter silence in the room as they re-assessed each other. The cat still lay on the table and continued to gaze implacably at Simon, who was struck once again by the resemblance between this animal and its master.

Simon felt oddly uneasy. It was a rare feeling and he did not like it. He sensed uncomfortably that he was not in complete control of the situation. Max, he had to admit, was an opponent with whom nothing should be taken for granted.

The Saint also got to his feet, seemingly as relaxed as ever but ready for instant action should his enemy make a move.

"Come on," he said, "let's cut the chat and get it over with."

Max and Thai continued to look at him. There was a queer light in the eyes of both of them. Simon could not read behind it, but all his senses were on the alert. He drew the flick knife from his pocket, and snapped it open.

"I hate to get melodramatic," he said, "but if you're thinking you can pull some kind of fast one, I promise you that I can throw this much faster."

"I would never try to compete with your expertise." It sounded almost as if the cat were purring Max's words. There was an aura which emanated from this man which was paradoxically both stimulating and lulling. "But I do have these qualities at my service, only they belong to another being."

"Your tame bully boys?"

Max's soft white hands stroked Thai.

"By the way, how did you get past them?"

"I came a different way. Now we'll go together—the regular way—and be as friendly as anything when we pass your guards." Simon made a movement with the knife to underline his meaning.

Max's eyes were wide and brilliant. He looked like a fat cat about to pounce. It was a greedy, anticipatory look, excited yet with a touch of fear.

The Saint had seen that look many times at gambling tables. It was the look of someone who expects to make a killing. Perhaps Annellatt was expecting just that. His body was utterly still except for the hand stroking Thai.

To Simon it seemed that time had stopped for a long moment. When it started again something would happen.

Then Max spoke.

"Get him, Thai," he commanded, and flung the cat at Simon.

3

Simon was suddenly immersed in a flurry of fur and tearing claws, which ripped at his face and neck in savage frenzy. He felt as if he were being attacked by a miniature tiger.

If Max himself or any other human being had attacked him like that, the Saint would have used his knife in an almost reflex action. Against a theoretically domestic pet, the thought patterns of a lifetime made it nearly as instinctive to hold back. And then, before he could overcome his reluctance to use the blade, the cat was gone, leaping through the half-open window. Simon never did discover where Thai went. It was possible that the animal simply leapt down into the courtyard. But that would have been a formidable jump even for a cat, but Thai was certainly no ordinary cat, and reminded him more of the feline "familiar" with which superstition used to credit witches.

Anyway, Simon was not concerned with Thai at that moment. It had vanished; but then, so had its master.

Max's disappearance was more prosaic. He had simply gone through the door. It was still open as he had left it.

Simon did not rush after him. He figured there would be many escape routes in the Castle, and Max would be well clear before pursuit even got started, while the Saint himself would risk blundering into an ambush. The man who had so admirably and cleverly outwitted him might well have more tricks up his sleeve now. It was not often that the Saint met his match.

What the future held for Max was something to speculate about another time. Simon imagined that such a successful and influential crook must have contacts in many countries. He would easily be able to build a new life for himself in some place like Argentina or Peru. Perhaps a peon in Columbia, sneaking a sackful of stolen gems from an emerald mine, would have merry brown eyes and hum "The Blue Danube" as he went. Or perhaps Max would be the subject of a Grand Jury investigation in New York. Simon wondered if they would let him wear Thai like a fur collar while he invoked the Fifth Amendment.

The Saint was more concerned with his immediate situation. He could, of course, walk out of Max's study and down the passage to the door which opened on to the gallery. As he knew, it was locked and possibly bolted on his side. Obviously the sensible thing to do was to go along and unlock it and walk back across the gallery to his room. But his room had also been locked by the indefatigable Erich, who had taken the key away, and the Saint had not brought any tools for lock-picking.

It seemed to him that for far too long he had been on the run from people intent on doing him harm. He was tired of having to crawl and climb around difficult, uncomfortable and even dangerous places, in order to elude this type of person. But then, up to now, he had been handicapped by having a young and impulsive woman to look after and an equally young and even more impulsive boy. Now he was on his own, which was how he liked it to be, and he decided to make the most of it.

Inspired by the thought, he stuffed the necklace casually into his shirt pocket and set off back down the stairs, treading as insouciantly as if he owned them.

Suddenly, from below came the sound of voices and feet running along the echoing passage. Max, en route to freedom, had alerted his bully boys and told them to go and get the Saint and do him in. That way he wouldn't be around when the ultimate nastiness took place, and his sensitive soul would remain unbruised.

Then Simon saw them, the Rat and the Gorilla, waiting for him at the foot of the stairs. Annellatt's men.

Being the obedient thick-headed villains they were, and being two to one, and armed, they must have figured they were in an impregnable position. They were like two well-trained and rather vicious dogs, and the Saint for an instant almost felt sorry for them. Until he remembered the surprised look on the dead face of Anton as he lay in a pool of his own blood in the cabin.

If the Rat and the Gorilla had the advantage of weaponry and numbers, Simon Templar had the advantage of surprise, which he could create for himself by sheer quickness of wit. And in such an emergency his wits connected like lightning.

"Geronimo!" he yelled, at the most startling top of his lungs, and did something which his adversaries could not possibly have dreamed of his doing in such circumstances. He simply leapt on to the banister and slid downwards.

The Gorilla's reflexes were too slow to enable him to take aim at such a fast-moving target. The Rat recovered faster, but by the time he had come out of shock sufficiently to bring his gun to bear, Simon had left the banisters halfway down and dropped from view on the floor below, and the Rat's bullet harmlessly splintered the rail.

The Saint was now concealed from the two thugs by the staircase itself, but he gave them no time to regroup. Whirling like an avenging typhoon around the newel post at the bottom of the stairs, he was upon the Rat before the latter could locate him. The Rat, being small and not particularly strong, didn't stand a chance, which was all the more unfortunate for him since the Saint used him as a shield between himself and the Gorilla, whose reactions were too sluggish to stop him pulling the trigger of the gun he was trying to aim at the Saint. That bullet ended the Rat's meager and evil-filled life for good and all—or perhaps, more aptly, for bad and all.

The Rat's pistol dropped from his dead hand, and the Rat followed it and cascaded on to the floor.

The Gorilla was still trying to take aim when the Saint threw his knife. The gun spoke, but the Gorilla's shot went wide because of the swiftness with which the Saint was moving. The knife flew straight and true as an arrow to bury itself up to the hilt in the Gorilla's throat, and the Gorilla slumped to the ground beside the Rat, choking his last gasps on his own blood.

The Saint did not wait to consider their passing, any longer than to scoop up the handiest of the two fallen guns. The two thugs, he considered, were better out of this world than in it.

His own tiredness had evaporated, the blood raced through his veins and zest filled his soul. He had done what he liked doing best, triumphing over the Ungodly and thwarting their knavish tricks, as the British National Anthem called them. So he told himself. Actually, if he had been more analytical, he would have been honest enough to admit that it boiled down to the fact that he had enjoyed a good fight and coming out on top.

Which was all very fine, except that winning a skirmish was not winning a war. Or even a decisive battle. There were still hurdles to take, bridges to cross, and even metaphors to mangle.

In plainer language, what was the back-up organisation behind the latest casualties? And/or what was the other factor which their clumsiness didn't fully account for?

Who tipped off the border guards about the fake passes? Who, in another phrase, was the rotten apple in Max Annellatt's own carefully sifted barrel?

Stepping over the prostrate bodies of his two erstwhile opponents, Simon walked down to the end of the passage where there were two doors. The one straight ahead obviously led into the main body of the Schloss, and he knew the one on the left gave on to the courtyard.

The Saint tried the inner door. As he expected, it was locked. Behind it, all the state rooms would also be locked and wired with burglar alarms.

Simon Templar believed that the most direct and obvious action was frequently the most brilliant. He therefore calmly unbolted the courtyard door and walked out into what still remained of the night.

As he moved briskly across the cobblestones, he checked the load and action of the gun he had taken over. One hazard he could do without was that of being penalised by any incompetence of the enemy, who in some respects had betrayed streaks of vulnerable sloppiness. He tucked the pistol under his belt, just inside the unbuttoned front of his shirt.

He mounted the broad steps to the main front door of the Castle, and rang the bell just as if he were a casual visitor—albeit a casual visitor with bloody scratches on his face. There was no answer, so the Saint rang again, this time long and hard.

After a while, the lights went up in the Great Hall and there was a noise of bolts being retracted. The lock clicked as the key turned, and then the door slowly and silently opened, the alarm having been switched off.

The Saint stepped into the blazingly lighted hall.

"Good evening—once again, Erich!" he said.

4

The manservant's eyes goggled and his jaw hung open. In a moment, however, he had regained his composure and his face once more wore its professional mask. In his hand was a Luger automatic, and Simon noted that it was held in a manner which combined decorum with instant readiness for action.

"Ach, Herr Templar!" Erich's eyes flicked as he tried to determine whether Simon was armed. "What has happened, sir? How do you come here?"

The Saint smiled genially.

"Locked doors do not a prison make, my dear Erich, to misquote a famous English poet."

The man's dark eyes became expressionless once again. The Saint sensed, as indeed he had always felt about Erich, that here was potentially a really dangerous customer, far above the calibre of the Rat and the Gorilla. Had the man possessed a sense of humour he might even have approached Max's stature in villainy. Even so, the Saint realised that he would have to be very careful in dealing with the humourless Erich.

"But what are you doing here, sir?" the man repeated. "I thought you had retired for the night."

"I had, but I'm given to sleep-walking, especially down the sides of buildings. The doctors tell me I'm a unique case. It only comes over me when I get close to Dracula country. Do you have any bats in your belfry?"

As he rambled on inconsequentially, the Saint was edging into the doorway. But Erich was not to be caught unawares. He stepped backwards, but his gun was still at the ready.

"You have not told me why you are here," he persisted stubbornly.

"And why I am not still locked in my room," said the Saint dryly. "But I have some bad news for you. Your master has vanished. I can't find him anywhere."

For an instant there was a glint of surprise in the other's eyes. Then his lids drooped partially over them.

"He is in his study, sir," he replied, giving the Saint a calculating stare.

"Oh, no, he isn't. I've just been up there."

"Impossible," Erich said flatly. "I have been in my quarters, and at this time of night the only entrance to the East Wing is past my room because the state rooms are all locked and their burglar alarm is switched on."

"Perhaps he turned himself into a bat," responded the Saint helpfully. "Or maybe he's been kidnapped. Didn't you hear a couple of shots a few minutes ago?"

As he spoke he again attempted to edge closer to Erich, but once more the manservant retreated, his gun held steadily on target.

"I was on my way to investigate them, sir, when you rang the bell."

"There seems to have been some sort of a fracas," Simon informed him. "There are a couple of dead men at the foot of the stairs in that wing. Someone seems to have been playing games rather roughly with them."

Erich's eyes widened.

"*Furchtbar!* Who are they, these men?"

The Saint was watching him keenly.

"I don't know their names, but I've seen them around before in other places, and they were never up to any good. One of them looks like a big ape and the other like a rat."

Erich's face was once more expressionless.

"Are you sure *you* did not kill them, sir?" His query was polite, but his voice had a menacing ring.

"No, I'm not," said the Saint cheerfully. "Or yes I am, whichever way you want to look at it. What I mean is, I am not sure I did not kill them because I did kill them."

Erich's eyes were suddenly as cold as agates. So was his voice.

"And possibly, sir, you have killed the Herr Baron?"

"No, he was too quick for me. I didn't get the chance. He

jumped on his cat and rode off between the chimney pots. A very versatile chap, your master."

Erich's gun pointed directly at the Saint's heart.

"What have you done with him?"

"I tell you," maintained the Saint, "I haven't touched the blighter. But his cat touched me in several places." He indicated the scratches on his face. "Left his calling card, he did."

"I think, Mr Templar, you had better answer my question."

"I have. Quite truthfully. Your master did a bunk. Or as they say in America, he took it on the lam. *Sie scheinen schwer von Begriff zu sein.* I expect he's in his car right now heading for parts unknown as fast as it will take him. Don't ask me which, any one will do for him in his present circumstances. He's a refugee from the Law, you see, as well as from me. You might be in a bit of the same trouble yourself, just from having been associated with him. Unless you'd claim that you were always really working for yourself—but that could be embarrassing too, couldn't it?"

"*Was meinen Sie?*"

"I mean that Max's beautiful organisation had its weak spot, like a lot of brilliant organisations have had before. As the old saying goes, a chain is only as strong as its weakest link. In this case, the weak link is you."

"*Ich verstehe nicht.*"

"Oh, but you do understand. Like a lot of smartie subordinates before you, you thought you were smarter than the Boss. So you thought you could use his set-up for a while, and then take over and ditch him at the right moment. It's only your bad luck that I got wise to the double-cross. Maybe you were just that much too clever when you tipped somebody off about our false papers."

For a while there was silence. Erich was obviously fitting the pieces of a jigsaw puzzle together, swiftly and competently, in his mind.

"I think," he said finally, "that I shall have to kill you."

The Saint actually laughed. A spectator would have thought that he was really enjoying himself. The spectator would have been right. This was just the sort of situation that Simon Templar revelled in: death only a few feet and perhaps only a few seconds away. Unless he could dodge it.

"I expect you're right," he said. "But I must warn you that I'm probably quicker on the draw and a better shot than you are. It's my Boy Scout training."

Erich steadied his aim deliberately. For a long moment they faced each other. Then the Saint dipped into his shirt pocket and brought out the necklace. The movement was slow and relaxed, making sure not to give any suggestion that he might be going for a concealed weapon. Which he was doing, of course; but this weapon was psychological.

Erich's eyes bulged as he saw the fiery splendour of the stones. Obviously his mother hadn't told him that artificial gems could sparkle as brightly as real ones. He drew in his breath sharply.

"*Das Halsband!*" he whispered, as if he were admitting something against his will. With an effort he switched back to English and his attention to Simon. "Where . . . how did you get it?"

The Saint swung the necklace in languid hypnotic arcs in front of the man's eyes, and Erich had difficulty in keeping his gaze from following it.

"Your master gave it to me," Simon answered. "He said he didn't want it any more—or you either. So off he went, leaving me to dispose of both of you."

Erich was not easily intimidated.

"In that case," he said, "you are wrong, Mr Templar. It is I who will dispose."

"Have it your own way," said the Saint accommodatingly. "But if this is what you want most, you're welcome to it. Help yourself—as one *Schmuck* to another."

And he tossed the Hapsburg necklace carelessly to the footman, even more carelessly than Max Annellatt had recently tossed it to him.

Adept as he was, Erich would scarcely have been human if he had not grabbed at the necklace as it snaked towards him. For one fatal instant his attention was distracted from the Saint.

That was all Simon needed. A moment suddenly seemed to elongate itself as he filled it with sudden action. Leaping across, he knocked the gun from Erich's hand and seized the servant's arm in a grip which should normally have compelled submission.

But the footman also knew some tricks of the trade. As the Saint began to apply the pressure on his captive arm which would have forced him to give in, Erich kicked him hard and accurately on the shin.

Simon was, after all, human, and a shin is a most painful portion of one's anatomy when it is struck a violent blow. For a moment his concentration also wavered, and Erich was as quick as the Saint had been to use that moment to his advantage, and while Simon's grip fractionally relaxed Erich wriggled free. He leapt back and looked around for his gun.

It lay on the floor, just out of his reach and even more out of Simon's.

Erich automatically dived for it, and the Saint just as automatically did not try to beat him to it. Instead, the Saint's right hand dived inside his shirt for the pistol that he had tucked away.

It was a moderately close thing, but in such circumstances moderation is more than enough.

"Well," said the Saint, more or less to himself, as Erich crumpled quite ummistakably out of active participation, "I suppose a devout cricketer would call this a hat trick."

VIII

How Simon Templar had the last word

1

"Only nobody in the cast," Simon continued to himself, in the same mournful vein, "ever seemed to wear a hat."

That line of reflection was mercifully terminated by the appearance on the landing above of Frankie and Leopold in their dressing-gowns.

"You can come down," said the Saint. "Everything's safe for now. But I'm afraid you missed all the fun."

The most perfunctory examination was enough to confirm that Erich would never take part in another crime, on his own or anyone else's behalf. It was the kind of permanent and incontestable reformation which the Saint found it easiest to believe in.

He tucked his gun away and picked up the necklace as Frankie and Leopold joined him.

"What has been going on?" Leopold demanded.

"And where did that come from?" Frankie demanded.

Simon handed the necklace to her with a bow.

"Max gave it to me. He asked me to pass it on to you with his love and a farewell kiss."

"Max?" She was completely bewildered. "How on earth . . . ? Where is he?"

"Probably on his way to the North Pole," said the Saint. "I expect he'll set up an igloo there, with a sign offering reindeer for hire and Christmas presents delivered. And God help your presents once they're in his sack."

The girl literally stamped her foot.

"Simon, if you don't stop your stupid jokes I shall kill you. What has happened?"

"Well, it's a bit long for a bedtime story," said the Saint. "But I suppose you'll never sleep if I don't tell it."

He made the telling as brief and concise as it could be without leaving any of their inevitable questions unanswered.

"And so," he concluded, "apart from the great Annellatt himself, the opposition seems to have been disposed of. The ghosts of our three other playmates, wherever they are, can only be comparing notes on how they got there. Which leaves us in the clear, so long as nobody connects us with that little misunderstanding at the frontier."

"But there are three dead men here," Leopold uttered, almost in disbelief.

"That's nothing compared with the last act of most of Shakespeare's plays," the Saint reassured him. "Anyhow, with a little rearrangement I think I can make it look as if they perished in a friendly shoot-out between themselves. At least convincingly enough to give the local *polizei* a reasonable excuse for not working themselves into exhaustion over it. Or it might even be amusing to pin the rap on this two-timing Jeeves."

Leopold dragged his eyes away from Erich's uninterested body.

"We shall have to call the police," he said conventionally.

"Not just yet," said the Saint. "I don't want to get involved. Let the Gestapo and the Austrian Sherlock-holmes-gesellschaft sweat it out between them."

Frankie looked again, somewhat blankly, at the necklace which she was holding as if she was still in a trance that had come on when the Saint gave it to her.

"And this?" she said. "If it is really an imitation—"

"I'm not interested in your family skeletons, whatever dungeons you keep them in," said the Saint curtly. "But even at this unearthly hour, I think we should be heading back to Vienna as soon as we can get organised, to set up any alibis that we might inconceivably need. As for the Hapsburg Necklace, the Keeper has it, or what's left to keep now. So I hope that closes the book."

"You are forgetting," Frankie said, "I gave my real name when I went to Schloss Este."

"That was an impostor," said the Saint. "Like the man in SS uniform who sprung her. It must all have been part of some fiendish Jewish plot, maybe to steal the necklace. But you never left Vienna. So let's pack up and hustle back there. This place is beginning to feel like a morgue."

2

They met that evening for a farewell supper at the Kursalon by Vienna's Stadtpark.

It was the Saint's idea. For one thing he liked the place, which was oldfashioned, romantically dusted with the atmosphere of the Hapsburg Empire, when it had been the scene of many an illicit amatory rendezvous. It still was, although its manner was less ostentatious and it seemed slightly anachronistic in the rather brutal climate of the times. Nevertheless, discreet waiters served one expertly and then left one alone, which made it just the place for a quiet talk in one of the cubicles it considerately provided for dallying couples.

Secondly, it was not an establishment frequented by high society. They could dine there, surrounded by chomping Viennese petite bourgeoisie, without the likelihood of being recognised. Not that the Saint was expecting trouble, but he did want them to be by themselves. At Sachers, Demmels, or any of the other smart restaurants or cafés, some friend of Frankie's or Leopold's might come up and, Viennese fashion, stay for a long gossip.

When they were seated in the secluded alcove and their orders had been taken by a waiter who gave the impression that he regarded culinary dishes as state secrets the Saint raised his cocktail glass.

"Here's to us, we three musketeers. All for one and one for all—and all for the Queen's Necklace that wasn't."

Frankie was looking marvellous in a dark blue dress shot with silver which did wonderful things for her figure and vice versa. The colour was a perfect foil for her raven hair and matched the brilliant blue of her eyes.

The Saint smiled at her.

"You look good enough to eat or something. Mostly something."

Leopold yawned involuntarily and seemed slightly guilty at having done so.

"Still tired?" asked the Saint. "I've been asleep all day in my hotel."

"So have I been asleep all day," said Leopold, "but I think I need at least a week."

"I only had a little sleep," said Frankie, "and I'm not tired at all. I had something to attend to—and then I bought this dress. Do you like it? I thought of you, Simon, when I chose it."

The Saint raised an eyebrow. The warning system which every confirmed bachelor always keeps switched on gave a faint signal.

"You'd better not think of me too often or you'll go broke."

"You are leaving tomorrow?" Leopold inquired pleasantly —but somewhat pointedly, the Saint thought.

"Yes—with much regret. It's been great fun, kids, but I must get back to real life. It's a bit hard to find it here in Austria."

"You cannot believe that," Frankie said.

Her eyes were big and full of meaning. Her perfume smelled expensive and expensively exciting, which just about summed up Frankie. It struck Simon that it might have been very pleasant to linger awhile in this *opera bouffe* country where dreams and reality were hard to distinguish and often were the same thing.

"Oh, I know we've seen some real death," he said. "But that isn't exactly what I meant."

"You really did risk your life," said the girl softly, "and I want to thank you for saving mine."

"Think nothing of it," Simon replied with careful lightness. "I'm always rescuing beautiful damsels in distress. I'm only sorry I'm not so good at saving necklaces."

"But you are!"

The Saint frowned.

"I must be a bit dense," he said. "But you'll have to explain that."

"You did save the Hapsburg Necklace. *The real one.*"

Simon felt that if Frankie hadn't lost her mind, he must be losing his. And Leopold's face testified that he was in the same condition.

"When was that?" Simon asked, with the kind of patience one employs to humour a maniac.

"Ever since you got me out of Schloss Este."

"And where is it now?"

"In a vault at Schöllers Bank. I put it there today."

"Do you mind telling us how, when and where you got it?" asked the Saint, with superhuman restraint.

"In Schloss Este, where I told you it was."

"But how?" demanded Leopold, almost frothing at the mouth.

"Very simple. It was in the dungeon where it was supposed to be."

"And the fake necklace?" asked the Saint. "Was that there too?"

She made a moue.

"Don't be silly. I took that with me, to be stolen, as I knew it might be."

The Saint inhaled long and deeply.

"Where did you hide the real one?"

"Attached to a cord around my waist, under my last petticoat."

At last he could only laugh.

"Well, we almost got down to it, didn't we?"

Leopold was shaking and his face had gone from red to white.

"You made a fool of me. That is one thing we Denksdorffs never permit."

Frankie's smile was wicked.

"Perhaps your family motto should be 'We only make fools of ourselves.'"

The Saint felt sorry for the young man. Frankie was being unnecessarily cruel.

The arrival of their first course, and the opening and tasting of a bottle of Willm Gewurztraminer, made a sorely needed interlude.

Frankie herself must have realised that she risked going too far. As soon as the waiters had dispersed again, she said: "Darling Leopold! You are behaving like a hero in a romantic novel."

He gave her a look which was filled with both love and hate.

"And you are behaving like a spoiled child!"

"I do think it's time you stopped tormenting us," Simon intervened peaceably. "So you were smart enough not to trust anybody. I can't say I blame you. But I'm sure it wasn't Leopold you were afraid of."

"I knew all along that Max was out to get the Necklace," she said.

"But it was you who introduced him to me," Leopold said.

She shrugged.

"Everyone in Austria knows he's a crook. Everyone but you, *mein Liebchen*. You are the original pure knight on a white charger. You do no evil and see no evil. But Max is a showpiece. That is why he is so popular in Austria. We like amusing rogues."

"But why did you allow him to become our partner then?"

"He was just the man I wanted. 'Set a thief to catch a thief' is an old proverb. But that works in another way too. You could say 'Set a thief to steal something!' Max had all the skills, crookedness, money and organisation that I needed. He lent us all of them—*nicht wahr?*"

The Saint could not help admiring this girl. She had caused him a lot of trouble but she certainly had what it took. It might indeed be pleasant to find out what it did take with her, just so long as he gave away nothing himself.

"You could have told me," Leopold said angrily.

"Yes, and I was afraid that if I did, my dear cousin, you might let the cat out of the bag. You are so impetuous."

"But what made you so sure that in the end you would be more clever than Max?"

"I was not altogether sure at first." Frankie's smile was shamelessly gamine. "But after I had the Saint on my side, I was sure."

Simon's admiration for this girl deepened. She was confirming much of what he had guessed, but he did not know many women who would have had the nerve and the gambler's instinct to act in the almost Saint-like way that she had all along.

He raised his glass to her again.

"I'm glad I was around," he murmured. "Well, so we go our various ways. And what's yours?"

"I'm going to the Semmering for a bit of skiing," she replied. "Wouldn't you like to come?" she added, batting her eyelashes at him provocatively.

"I'd love to, but with Schicklgruber in the saddle there may be more serious things to think about." He turned to Leopold. "And what are your plans?"

The young man's eyes were wide and almost desperate.

"I am going to marry Frankie," he announced thunderously, as if he were an archduke declaring a bazaar open. "She needs to be settled down."

"I hope you can do it for her," said the Saint. "I can't imagine a better match. The fact that she is twenty years older than you shouldn't be any handicap at all."

Leopold looked at him in amazement.

"What do you mean? We are practically the same age."

"All women are twenty years older than any man."

Frankie blew Simon a kiss.

"Except you." Her eyes met the Saint's steadily. "I wonder if you will meet Max Annellatt again one day. He would certainly be disguised."

"I'll still recognise him," said the Saint, "if he's wearing his old school Thai."

WATCH FOR THE SIGN
OF THE SAINT

HE WILL BE BACK